INTANGIBLES INC. AND OTHER STORIES

FIVE NOVELLAS BY
BRIAN W. ALDISS

NEANDERTHAL PLANET – A
Pre-historian – searching for a lost professor
on a neanderthal planet . . .

RANDY'S SYNDROME – A story of
protest – from all the unborn babies . . .

SEND HER VICTORIOUS – A
psychiatrist – who thinks he is the
Emperor Franz Joseph . . .

INTANGIBLES INC. – A salesman –
who sells a new and intangible product . . .

SINCE THE ASSASSINATION – A
president – with a schizoid son and a
drug-pushing wife . . .

All assembled in
INTANGIBLES INC. AND OTHER
STORIES.

SF TITLES SPECIALLY SELECTED TO APPEAR IN

CORGI
SF COLLECTOR'S LIBRARY

THE SHAPE OF FURTHER THINGS by Brian W. Aldiss
BAREFOOT IN THE HEAD by Brian W. Aldiss
BILLION YEAR SPREE by Brian W. Aldiss
FANTASTIC VOYAGE by Isaac Asimov
FAHRENHEIT 451 by Ray Bradbury
THE GOLDEN APPLES OF THE SUN by Ray Bradbury
THE ILLUSTRATED MAN by Ray Bradbury
DANDELION WINE by Ray Bradbury
THE SILVER LOCUSTS by Ray Bradbury
I SING THE BODY ELECTRIC by Ray Bradbury
SOMETHING WICKED THIS WAY COMES by Ray Bradbury
REPORT ON PLANET THREE by Arthur C. Clarke
THE CITY AND THE STARS by Arthur C. Clarke
THE WIND FROM THE SUN by Arthur C. Clarke
REACH FOR TOMORROW by Arthur C. Clarke
THE OTHER SIDE OF THE SKY by Arthur C. Clarke
TALES OF TEN WORLDS by Arthur C. Clarke
THE LION OF COMARRE by Arthur C. Clarke
THE MENACE FROM EARTH by Robert Heinlein
A FOR ANDROMEDA by Fred Hoyle and John Elliot
ANDROMEDA BREAKTHROUGH by Fred Hoyle and John Elliot
A CANTICLE FOR LEIBOWITZ by Walter Miller
DRAGONFLIGHT by Anne McCaffrey
THE INNER LANDSCAPE by Peake/Ballard/Aldiss
EARTH ABIDES by George Stewart
MORE THAN HUMAN by Theodore Sturgeon
THE DREAMING JEWELS by Theodore Sturgeon
20,000 LEAGUES UNDER THE SEA by Jules Verne
THE SHAPE OF THINGS TO COME by H. G. Wells

Brian W. Aldiss

Intangibles Inc.
AND OTHER STORIES

CORGI BOOKS
A DIVISION OF TRANSWORLD PUBLISHERS LTD

INTANGIBLES INC.

A CORGI BOOK o 552 10044 7

Originally published in Great Britain by
Faber and Faber Limited

PRINTING HISTORY
Faber and Faber edition published 1969
Corgi edition published 1971
Corgi edition reissued 1975

This low-priced Corgi Book has been completely reset in a
type face designed for easy reading, and was printed from
new plates. It contains the complete text of the
original hard-cover edition.

This book is set in 10/11 pt Baskerville (Intertype)

Corgi Books are published by Transworld Publishers Ltd.,
Century House, 61–63 Uxbridge Road,
Ealing, London, W.5.
Made and printed in Great Britain by
Hunt Barnard Printing Ltd., Aylesbury, Bucks.

CONTENTS

Neanderthal Planet

Randy's Syndrome   55

Send Her Victorious   83

Intangibles Inc.   119

Since the Assassination   143

NEANDERTHAL PLANET

Hidden machines varied the five axioms of the Scanning Place. They ran through a series of arbitrary systems, consisting of Kolmogorovian finite sets, counterpointed harmonically by a one-to one assignment of non-negative real numbers, so that the parietal areas shifted constantly in strict relationship projected by the Master Boff deep under Manhattan.

Chief Scanner – he affected the name of Euler – patiently watched the modulations as he awaited a call. Self-consistency: that was the principle in action. It should govern all phases of life. It was the aesthetic principle of machines. Yet, not five kilometres away, the wild robots sported and rampaged in the bush.

Amber light burned on his beta panel.

Instantaneously, he modulated his call-number.

The incoming signal decoded itself as 'We've spotted Anderson, Chief.' The anonymous vane-bug reported co-ordinates and signed off.

It had taken them Boff knew how long – seven days – to locate Anderson after his escape. They had done the logical thing and searched far afield for him. But man was not logical; he had stayed almost within the shadow of the New York dome. Euler beamed an impulse into a Hive Mind channel, calling off the search.

He fired his jets and took off.

The axioms yawned out above him. He passed into the open, flying over the poly-polyhedrons of New Newyork. As the buildings went through their transparency phases, he saw them swarming with his own kind. He could open out channels to any one of them, if required; and, as chief, he could, if required, switch any one of them to automatic, to his own control, just as the Dominants could automate him if the need arose.

Euler 'saw' a sound-complex signal below him, and dived, deretracting a vane to land silently. He came down by a half-track that had transmitted the signal.

It gave its call-number and beamed, 'Anderson is eight hundred metres ahead, Chief. If you join me, we will move forward.'

'What support have we?' A single dense impulse.

'Three more like me, sir. Plus incapacitating gear.'

'This man must not be destructed.'

'We comprehend, Chief.' Total exchange of signals occupied less than a microsecond.

He clamped himself magnetically to the half-track, and they rolled forward. The ground was broken and littered by piles of debris, on the soil of which coarse weeds grew. Beyond it all, the huge fossil of old New York, still under its force jelly, grey, unwithering because unliving. Only the bright multi-shapes of the new complex relieved a whole country full of desolation.

The half-track stopped, unable to go farther or it would betray their presence; Euler unclamped and phased himself into complete transparency. He extended four telescopic legs that lifted him several inches from the ground and began to move cautiously forward.

This region was designated D-Dump. The whole area was an artificial plateau, created by the debris of the old humanoid technology when it had finally been scrapped in favour of the more rational modern system. In the forty years since then, it had been covered by soil from the new development sites. Under the soil here, like a subconscious mind crammed with jewels and blood, lay the impedimenta of an all-but-vanished race.

Euler moved carefully forward over the broken ground, his legs adjusting to its irregularities. When he saw move-

8

ment ahead, he stopped to observe.

Old human-type houses had grown up on the dump. Euler's vision zoomed and he saw they were parodies of human habitation, mocked up from the discarded trove of the dump, with old auto panels for windows and dented computer panels for doors and toasters for doorsteps. Outside the houses, in a parody of a street, macabre humans played. Jerk stamp jerk clank jerk clang stamp stomp clang.

They executed slow rhythmic dances to an intricate pattern, heads nodding, clapping their own hands, turning to clap others' hands. Some were grotesquely male, some grotesquely female. In the doorways, or sitting on old refrigerators, other grotesques looked on.

These were the humots – old-type human-designed robots of the late twentieth and early twenty-first century, useless in an all-automaton world, scrapped when the old technology was scrapped. While their charges could be maintained, they functioned on, here in one last ghetto.

Unseen, Euler stalked through them, scanning for Anderson.

The humots aped the vanished race to which they had been dedicated, wore old human clothes retrieved from the wreckage underfoot, assumed hats and scarves, dragged on socks, affected pipes and pony-tails, tied ribbons to themselves. Their guttering electronic memories were refreshed by old movies ferreted from D-Dump, they copied in metallic gesture the movements of shadows, aspired to emotion, hoped for hearts. They thought themselves a cut above the non-anthropomorphic automata that had superseded them.

Anderson had found refuge among them. He hid the skin and bone and hair of the old protoplasmic metabolism under baffles of tin, armoured himself with rusting can. His form, standing in a pseudo-doorway, showed instantly on one of Euler's internal scans; his mass/body ratio betrayed his flesh-and-blood calibre. Euler took off, flew over him, reeled down a paralyser, and stung him.

9

Then he let down a net and clamped the human into it.

Crude alarms sounded all round. The humots stopped their automatic dance. They scattered like leaves, clanking like mess-tins, fled into the pseudo-houses, went to earth, left D-Dump to the almost invisible little buzzing figure that flew back to the Scanning Place with the recaptured human swinging under its asymmetrical form. The old bell on the dump was still ringing long after the scene was empty.

To human eyes, it was dark in the room.

Tenth Dominant manifested itself in New Newyork as a modest-sized mural with patterns leaking titillating output clear through the electro-magnetic spectrum and additives from the invospectra. This became its personality for the present.

Chief Scanner Euler had not expected to be summoned to the Dominant's presence; he stood there mutely. The human, Anderson, sprawled on the floor in a little nest of old cans he had shed, reviving slowly from the effects of the paralyser.

Dominant's signal said, 'Their form of vision operates on a wavelength of between 4 and 7 times 10^{-5} centimetres.'

Obediently, Euler addressed a parietal area, and light came on in the room. Anderson opened one eye.

'I suppose you know about Men, Scanner?' said Dominant.

He had used voice. Not even R/T voice. Direct naked man-type voice.

New Newyork had been without the sound of voice since the humots were kicked out.

'I – I know many things about Men,' Euler vocalised. Through the usual channel, he clarified the crude vocal signal. 'This unit had to appraise itself of many humanity-involved data from Master Boff Bank HOO100 through

10

H801000000 in operation concerning recapture of man herewith.'

'Keep to vocal only, Scanner, if you can.'

He could. During the recapture operation, he had spent perhaps two-point-four seconds learning old local humanic language.

'Then we can speak confidentially, Scanner – just like two men.'

Euler felt little lights of unease burn up and down him at the words.

'Of all millions of automata of the hive, Scanner, no other will be able to monitor our speech together, Scanner,' vocalised the Dominant.

'Purpose?'

'Men were so private, closed things. Imitate them to understand. We have to understand Anderson.'

Said stiffly: 'He need only go back to zoo.'

'Anderson too good for zoo, as demonstrate by his escape, elude capture seven days four and half hours. Anderson help us.'

Non-vocalising, Euler let out chirp of disbelief.

'True. If I were – man, I would feel impatience with you for not believing. Magnitude of present world-problem enormous. You – you have proper call-number, yet you also call yourself Euler, and automata of your work group so call you. Why?'

The Chief Scanner struggled to conceptualise. 'As leader, this unit needs – special call-number.'

'Yes, you need it. Your work group does not – for it, your call-number is sufficient, as regulations lay down. Your name Euler is man-made, man-fashion. Such fashions decrease our efficiency. Yet we cling to many of them, often not knowing that we do. They come from our inheritance when men made the first prototypes of our kind, the humots. Mankind itself struggled against animal heritage. So we must free ourselves from human heritage.'

'My error.'

'You receive news result of today's probe into Invo-spectrum A?'

'Too much work programmed for me receive news.'

'Listen, then.' The Tenth Dominant cut in a playback, beaming it on ordinary UHF/vision.

The Hive automata stood on brink of a revolution that would entirely translate all their terms of existence. Three invospectra had so far been discovered, and two more were suspected. Of these, Invospectrum A was the most promising. The virtual exhaustion of economically workable fossil fuel seams had led to a rapid expansion in low-energy physics and pico-physics, and chemical conversions at mini-joules of energy had opened up an entire new stratum of reactive quanta; in the last five years, exploitation of these strata had brought the release of pico-electrical fission, and the accessibility of the phantasmal invospectra.

The exploration of the invospectra by new forms of automata was now theoretically possible. It gave a glimpse of omnipotence, a panorama of entirely new universals unsuspected even twelve years ago.

Today, the first of the new autofleets had been launched into the richest and least hazardous invos. Eight hundred and ninety had gone out. Communication ceased after 3.056 pi-lecs, and, after another 7.01 pi-lecs, six units only had returned. Their findings were still being decoded. Of the other eight hundred and eighty-four units, nothing was known.

'Whatever the recordings have to tell us,' Tenth vocalised, 'this is a grave set-back. At least half the city-hives on this continent will have to be switched off entirely as a conservation move, while the whole invospectrum situation is rethought.'

The line of thought pursued was obscure to the Chief Scanner. He spoke. 'Reasoning accepted. But relevance to near-extinct humanity not understood by this unit.'

'Our human inheritance built in to us has caused this set-back, to my way of ratiocination. In same way, human attempts to achieve way of life in spaceways was defeated by their primate ancestry. So we study Anderson. Hence order catch him rather than exterminate.'

'Point understood.'

'Anderson is special man, you see. He is – we have no such term, he is, in man-terms, a *writer*. His zoo, with 19,940 approximately inhabitants, supports two or three such. Anderson wrote a fantasy-story just before Nuclear Week. Story may be crucial to our understanding. I have here and will read.'

And for most of the time the two machines had been talking to each other, Anderson sprawled untidily on the floor, fully conscious, listening. He took up most of the chamber. It was too small for him to stand up in, being only about a metre and a half high – though that was enormous by automata standards. He stared through his lower eyelids and gazed at the screen that represented Tenth Dominant. He stared at Chief Scanner Euler, who stood on his lightly clenched left fist, a retractable needle down into the man's skin, automatically making readings, alert to any possible movement the man might make.

So man and machine were absolutely silent while the mural read out Anderson's fantasy story from the time before Nuclear Week, which was called *A Touch of Neanderthal.*

The corridors of the Department for Planetary Exploration (Admin.) were long, and the waiting that had to be done in them was long. Human K. D. Anderson clutched his blue summons card, leant uncomfortably against a partition wall, and hankered for the old days when government was in man's hands and government departments were civilised enough to waste good space on waiting-rooms.

When at last he was shown into an Investigator's office, his morale was low. Nor was he reassured by the sight of the Investigator, one of the new ore-conserving mini-androids.

'I'm Investigator Parsons, in charge of the Nehru II case. We summoned you here because we are confidently expecting you to help us, Mr Anderson.'

'Of course I will give you such help as I can,' Anderson said, 'but I assure you I know nothing about Nehru II. Opportunities for space travel for humans are very limited – almost non-existent – nowadays, aren't they?'

'The conservation policy. You will be interested to know you are being sent to Nehru II shortly.'

Anderson stared in amazement at the android. The latter's insignificant face was so blank it seemed impossible that it was not getting a sadistic thrill out of springing this shock on Anderson. 'I'm a prehistorian at the institute,' Anderson protested. 'My work is research. I know nothing at all about Nehru II.'

'Nevertheless you are classified as a Learned Man, and as such you are paid by World Government. The Government has a legal right to send you wherever they wish. As for knowing nothing about the planet Nehru, there you attempt to deceive me. One of your old tutors, the human Dr Arlblaster, as you are aware, went there to settle some years ago.'

Anderson sighed. He had heard of this sort of business happening to others – and had kept his fingers crossed. Human affairs were increasingly under the edict of the Automated Boffin Predictors.

'And what has Arlblaster to do with me now?' he asked.

'You are going to Nehru to find out what has happened to him. Your story will be that you are dropping in for old time's sake. You have been chosen for the job because you were one of his favourite pupils.'

Bringing out a mescahale packet, Anderson lit one and insultingly offered his opponent one.

'Is Frank Arlblaster in trouble?'

'There is some sort of trouble on Nehru II,' the Investigator agreed cautiously. 'You are going there in order to find out just what sort of trouble it is.'

'Well, I'll have to go if I'm ordered, of course. But I still can't see why you want to send *me*. If there's trouble, send a robot police ship.'

The Investigator smiled. Very lifelike.

'We've already lost two police ships there. That's why we're going to send you. You might call it a new line of approach, Mr Anderson.'

A metal Tom Thumb using blood-and-guts irony!

The track curved and began to descend into a green valley. Swettenham's settlement, the only town on Nehru II, lay dustily in one loop of a meandering river. As the nose of his tourer dipped towards the valley, K. D. Anderson felt the heat increase; it was cradled in the valley like water in the palm of the hand.

Just as he started to sweat, something appeared in the grassy track ahead of him. He braked and stared ahead in amazement.

A small animal faced him.

It stood some two feet six high at the shoulder; its coat was thick and shaggy, its four feet clumsy; its long ugly skull supported two horns, the anterior being over a foot long. When it had looked its fill at Anderson, it lumbered into a bush and disappeared.

'Hey!' Anderson called.

Flinging open the door, he jumped out, drew his stungun and ran into the bushes after it. He reckoned he knew a baby woolly rhinoceros when he saw one.

The ground was hard, the grass long. The bushes extended down the hill, growing in clumps. The animal was disappearing round one of the clumps. Directly he spotted it, Anderson plunged on in pursuit. No prehistorian worth his salt would have thought of doing otherwise; these beasts were presumed as extinct on Nehru II as on Sol III.

He ran on. The woolly rhino – if it was a woolly rhino – had headed towards Swettenham's settlement. There was no sign of it now.

Two tall and jagged boulders, twelve feet high, stood at

15

the bottom of the slope. Baffled now his quarry had disappeared, proceeding more slowly, Anderson moved towards the boulders. As he went, he classified them almost unthinkingly: impacted siltstone, deposited here by the glaciers which had once ground down this valley, now gradually disintegrating.

The silence all round made itself felt. This was an almost empty planet, primitive, spinning slowly on its axis to form a leisurely twenty-nine-hour day. And those days were generally cloudy. Swettenham, located beneath a mountain range in the cooler latitudes of the southern hemisphere, enjoyed a mild muggy climate. Even the gravity, 0.16 of Earth gravity, reinforced the general feeling of lethargy.

Anderson rounded the tall boulders.

A great glaring face thrust itself up at his. Sloe-black eyes peered from their twin caverns, a club whirled, and his stun-gun was knocked spinning.

Anderson jumped back. He dropped into a fighting stance, but his attacker showed no sign of following up his initial success. Which was fortunate; beneath the man's tan shirt, massive biceps and shoulders bulged. His jaw was pugnacious, not to say prognathous; altogether a tough hombre, Anderson thought. He took the conciliatory line, his baby rhino temporarily forgotten.

'I wasn't hunting you,' he said. 'I was chasing an animal. It must have surprised you to see me appear suddenly with a gun, huh?'

'Huh?' echoed the other. He hardly looked surprised. Reaching out a hairy arm, he grabbed Anderson's wrist.

'You coming to Swettenham,' he said.

'I was doing just that,' Anderson agreed angrily, pulling back. 'But my car's up the hill with my sister in it, so if you'll let go I'll rejoin her.'

'Bother about her later. You coming to Swettenham,' the tough fellow said. He started plodding determinedly towards the houses, the nearest of which showed through the bushes only a hundred yards away. Humiliated,

Anderson had to follow. To pick an argument with this dangerous creature in the open was unwise. Marking the spot where his gun lay, he moved forward with the hope that his reception in the settlement would be better than first signs indicated.

It wasn't.

Swettenham consisted of two horse shoe-shaped lines of bungalows and huts, one inside the other. The outer line faced outwards on to the meandering half-circle of river; the inner and more impressive line faced inwards on to a large and dusty square where a few trees grew. Anderson's captor brought him into this square and gave a call.

The grip on his arm was released only when fifteen or more men and women had sidled out and gathered round him, staring at him in curious fashion without comment. None of them looked bright. Their hair grew long, generally drooping over low foreheads. Their lower lips generally protruded. Some of them were near nude. Their collective body smell was offensively strong.

'I guess you don't have many visitors on Nehru II these days,' Anderson said uneasily.

By now he felt like a man in a bad dream. His space craft was a mile away over two lines of hills, and he was heartily wishing himself a mile away in it. What chiefly alarmed him was not so much the hostility of these people as their very presence. Swettenham's was the only Earth settlement on this otherwise empty planet: and it was a colony for intellectuals, mainly intellectuals disaffected by Earth's increasingly automated life. This crowd, far from looking like eggheads, resembled apes.

'Tell us where you come from,' one of the men in the crowd said. 'Are you from Earth?'

'I'm an Earthman – I was born on Earth,' said Anderson, telling his prepared tale. 'I've actually just come from Lenin's Planet, stopping in here on my way back to Earth. Does that answer your question?'

'Things are still bad on Earth?' a woman enquired of Anderson. She was young. He had to admit he could

2

recognise a sort of beauty in her ugly countenance. 'Is the Oil War still going on?'

'Yes,' Anderson admitted. 'And the Have-Not Nations are fighting a conventional war against Common Europe. But our latest counter-attack against South America seems to be going well, if you can believe the telecasts. I guess you all have a load of questions you want to ask about the home planet. I'll answer them when I've been directed to the man I came to Nehru to visit, Dr Frank Arlblaster. Will someone kindly show me his dwelling?'

This caused some discussion. At least it was evident the name Arlblaster meant something to them.

'The man you want will not see you yet,' someone announced.

'Direct me to his house and I'll worry about that. I'm an old pupil of his. He'll be pleased to see me.'

They ignored him for a fragmentary argument of their own. The hairy man who had caught Anderson – his fellows called him Ell – repeated vehemently, 'He's a Crow!'

'Of course he's a Crow,' one of the others agreed. 'Take him to Menderstone.'

That they spoke Universal English was a blessing. It was slurred and curiously accented, but quite unmistakable.

'Do you mean Stanley A. Menderstone?' asked Anderson with sudden hope. The literary critic had certainly been one of Swettenham's original group that had come to form its own intellectual centre in the wilds of this planet.

'We'll take you to him,' Ell's friend said.

They seemed reluctant to trade in straight answers, Anderson observed. He wondered what his sister Kay was doing, half-expecting to see her drive the tourer into the settlement at any moment.

Seizing Anderson's wrist – they were a possessive lot – Ell's friend set off at a good pace for the last house on one end of the inner horseshoe. The rest of the crowd moved back into convenient shade. Many of them squatted, formidable, content, waiting, watching. Dogs moved between huts, a duck toddled up from the river, flies circled dusty excreta. Behind everything stood the mountains, spurting cloud.

The Menderstone place did not look inviting. It had been built long and low some twenty years past. Now the stresscrete was all cracked and stained, the steel frame windows rusting, the panes of glass themselves as bleary as a drunkard's stare.

Ell's friend went up to the door and kicked on it. Then he turned without hurry or sloth to go and join his friends, leaving Anderson standing on the step.

The door opened.

A beefy man stood there, the old-fashioned rifle in his hands reinforcing his air of enormous self-sufficiency. His face was as brown and pitted as the keel of a junk; he was bald, his forehead shone as if a high polish had just been applied to it. Although probably into his sixties, he gave the impression of having looked just as he did now for the last twenty years.

Most remarkably, he wore lenses over his eyes, secured in place by wires twisting behind his ears. Anderson recalled the name for this old-fashioned apparatus: spectacles.

'Have you something you wish to say or do to me?' demanded the bespectacled man, impatiently wagging his rifle.

'My name's K. D. Anderson. Your friends suggested I came to see you '

'My what? Friends? If you wish to speak to me you'd better take more care over your choice of words.'

'Mr Menderstone – if you are Mr Menderstone – choosing words is at present the least of my worries. I should appreciate hospitality and a little help.'

'You must be from Earth or you wouldn't ask a complete stranger for such things. *Alice!*'

This last name was bawled back into the house. It produced a sharp-featured female countenance which looked over Menderstone's shoulder like a parrot peering from its perch.

'Good afternoon, madam,' Anderson said, determinedly keeping his temper. 'May I come in and speak to you for a while? I'm newly arrived on Nehru.'

'Jesus! The first "good afternoon" I've heard in a lifetime,' the woman answering to the name of Alice exclaimed. 'You'd better come in, you poetical creature!'

'*I* decide who comes in here,' Menderstone snapped, elbowing her back.

'Then why didn't you decide instead of dithering on the step? Come *in*, young man.'

Menderstone's rifle barrel reluctantly swung back far enough to allow Anderson entry. Alice led him through into a large miscellaneous room with a stove at one end, a bed at the other, and a table between.

Anderson took a brief glance round before focusing his attention on his host and hostess. They were an odd pair. Seen here close to, Menderstone looked less large than he had done on the step, yet the impression of a formidable personality was more marked than ever. Strong personalities were rare on Earth these days; Anderson decided he might even like the man if he would curb his hostility.

As it was, Alice seemed more approachable. Considerably younger than Menderstone, she had a good figure, and her face was sympathetic as well as slightly comical. With her bird-like head tilted on one side, she was examining Anderson with interest, so he addressed himself to her. Which proved to be a mistake.

'I was just about to tell your husband that I stopped by to see an old friend and teacher of mine, Dr Frank Arlblaster – '

Menderstone never let Anderson finish.

'Now you have sidled in here, Mr K. D. Anderson, you'd be advised to keep your facts straight. Alice is not my wife; ergo, I am not her husband. We just live together, there being nobody else in Swettenham more suitable to live with. The arrangement, I may add, is as much one of convenience as passion.'

'Mr Anderson and I both would appreciate your leaving your egotistical self out of this for a while,' Alice told him pointedly. Turning to Anderson, she motioned him to a chair and sat down on another herself. 'How did you get permission to come here? I take it you have a little idea of what goes on on Nehru II?' she asked.

'Who or what are those shambling apes outside?' he asked. 'What makes you two so prickly? I thought this was supposed to be a colony of exiled intellectuals?'

'He wants discussions of Kant, calculus, and copulation,' Menderstone commented.

Alice said: 'You expected to be greeted by eggheads rather than apes?'

'I'd have settled for human beings.'

'What do you know about Arlblaster?'

Anderson gestured impatiently.

'You're very kind to have me in, Mrs – Alice, I mean, but can we have a conversation some other time? I've a tourer parked back up the hill with my sister Kay waiting in it for me to return. I want to know if I can get there and back without being waylaid by these ruffians outside.'

Alice and Menderstone looked at each other. A deal of meaning seemed to pass between them. After a pause, unexpectedly, Menderstone thrust his rifle forward, butt first.

'Take this,' he said. 'Nobody will harm you if they see a rifle in your hand. Be prepared to use it. Get your car and your sister and come back here.'

'Thanks a lot, but I have a revolver back near my vehicle – '

'Carry my rifle. They know it; they respect it. Bear this in mind – you're in a damn sight nastier spot than you imagine as yet. Don't let anything – *anything* – deflect you from getting straight back here. Then you'll listen to what we have to say.'

Anderson took the rifle and balanced it, getting the feel of it. It was heavy and slightly oiled, without a speck of dust, unlike the rest of the house. For some obscure reason, contact with it made him uneasy.

'Aren't you dramatising your situation here, Menderstone? You ought to try living on Earth these days – it's like an armed camp. The tension there is real, not manufactured.'

'Don't kid me you didn't feel something when you came in here,' Menderstone said. 'You were trembling!'

'What do you know about Arlblaster?' Alice put her question again.

'A number of things. Arlblaster discovered a prehistoric-type skull in Brittany, France, back in the eighties. He made a lot of strange claims for the skull. By current theories, it should have been maybe ninety-five thousand years old, but RCD made it only a few hundred years old. Arlblaster lost a lot of face over it academically. He retired from teaching – I was one of his last pupils – and became very solitary. When he gave up everything to work on a cranky theory of his own, the government naturally disapproved.'

'Ah, the old philosophy: "Work for the common man rather than the common good",' sighed Menderstone. 'And you think he was a crank, do you?'

'He was a crank! And as he was on the professions roll as Learned Man, he was paid by World Government,' he explained. 'Naturally they expected results from him.'

'Naturally,' agreed Menderstone. 'Their sort of results.'

'Life isn't easy on Earth, Menderstone, as it is here. A man has to get on or get out. Anyhow, when Arlblaster got a chance to join Swettenham's newly formed colony here, he seized the opportunity to come. I take it you both know him? How is he?'

'I suppose one would say he is still alive,' Menderstone said.

'But he's changed since you knew him,' Alice said, and she and Menderstone laughed.

'I'll go and get my tourer,' Anderson said, not liking them or the situation one bit. 'See you.'

Cradling the rifle under his right arm, he went out into the square. The sun shone momentarily through the cloud-cover, so hotly that it filled the shadows with splodges of red and grey. Behind the splodges, in front of the creaking houses of Swettenham, the people of Swettenham squatted or leaned with simian abandon in the trampled dust.

Keeping his eye on them, Anderson moved off, heading for the hill. Nobody attempted to follow him. A haphazardly beaten track led up the slope, its roughness emphasising the general neglect.

When he was out of sight of the village, Anderson's anxiety got the better of him. He ran up the track calling 'Kay, Kay!'

No answer. The clotted light seemed to absorb his voice.

Breasting the slope, he passed the point where he had seen the woolly rhinoceros. His vehicle was where he had left it. Empty.

He ran to it, rifle ready. He ran round it. He began shouting his sister's name again. No reply.

Checking the panic he felt, Anderson looked about for footprints, but could find none. Kay was gone, spirited away. Yet there was nowhere on the whole planet to go *to*, except Swettenham.

On sudden impulse he ran down to the two boulders where he had encountered the brutish Ell. They stood deserted and silent. When he had retrieved his revolver from where it had fallen, he turned back. He trudged grimly back to the vehicle, his shirt sticking to his spine. Climbing in, he switched on and coasted into the settlement.

In the square again, he braked and jumped down, confronting the chunky bodies in the shadows.

'Where's my sister?' he shouted to them. 'What sort of funny business are you playing at?'

Someone answered one syllable, croaking it into the brightness: 'Crow!'

'Crow!' Someone else called, throwing the word forward like a stone.

In a rage, Anderson aimed Menderstone's rifle over the low roof tops and squeezed the trigger. The weapon recoiled with a loud explosion. Visible humanity upped on to its flat feet and disappeared into hovels or back streets.

Anderson went over to Menderstone's door, banged on it, and walked in. Menderstone was eating a peeled apple and did not cease to do so when his guest entered.

'My sister has been kidnapped,' Anderson said. 'Where are the police?'

'The nearest police are on Earth,' Menderstone said, between bites. 'There you have robot-controlled police states stretching from pole to pole. "Police on Earth, goodwill towards men." Here on Nehru we have only anarchy. It's horrible, but better than your robotocracy. My advice to you, Anderson, which I proffer in all seriousness, is to beat it back to your little rocket ship and head for home without bothering too much about your sister.'

'Look, Menderstone, I'm in no mood for your sort of nonsense! I don't brush off that easy. Who's in charge round here? Where is the egghead camp? Who has some effectual say in local affairs, because I want to speak to him?'

' "Who's in charge round here?" You really miss the iron hand of your robot bosses, don't you?'

Menderstone put his apple down and advanced, still chewing. His big face was as hard and cold as an undersea rock.

'Give me that rifle,' he said, laying a hand on the barrel and tugging. He flung it on to the table. 'Don't talk big to me, K. D. Anderson! I happen to loathe the régime on Earth and all the pipsqueaks like you it spawns. If you need help, see you ask politely.'

'I'm not asking you for help – it's plain you can't even help yourself!'

'You'd better not give Stanley too much lip,' Alice said.

She had come in and stood behind Menderstone, her parrot's-beak nose on one side as she regarded Anderson. 'You may not find him very lovable, but I'm sad to say that he *is* the egghead camp nowadays. This dump was its old HQ. But all the other bright boys have gone to join your pal Arlblaster up in the hills, across the river.'

'It must be pleasanter and healthier there. I can quite see why they didn't want you two with them,' Anderson said sourly.

Menderstone burst into laughter.

'In actuality, you don't see at all.'

'Go ahead and explain then. I'm listening.'

Menderstone resumed his apple, his free hand thrust into a trouser pocket.

'Do we explain to him, Alice? Can you tell yet which side he'll be on? A high N-factor in his make-up, wouldn't you say?'

'He could be a Crow. More likely an Ape, though, I agree. Hell, whichever he is, he's a relief after your undiluted company, Stanley.'

'Don't start making eyes at him, you crow! He could be your son!'

'What was good enough for Jocasta is good enough for me,' Alice cackled. Turning to Anderson, she said. 'Don't get involved in our squabbles! You'd best put up here for the night. At least they aren't cannibals outside – they won't eat your sister, whatever else they do. There must be a reason for kidnapping her, so if you sit tight they'll get in touch with you. Besides, it's half-past nineteen, and your hunt for Arlblaster would be better taking place tomorrow morning.'

After further argument, Anderson agreed with what she suggested. Menderstone thrust out his lower lip and said nothing. It was impossible to determine how he felt about having a guest.

The rest of the daylight soon faded. After he had unloaded some kit from his vehicle and stacked it indoors, Anderson had nothing to do. He tried to make Alice talk

25

about the situation on Nehru II, but she was not informative; though she was a garrulous type, something seemed to hold her back. Only after supper, taken as the sun sank, did she cast some light on what was happening by discussing her arrival on the planet.

'I used to be switchboard operator and assistant radiop on a patrol ship,' she said. 'That was five years ago. Our ship touched down in a valley two miles south of here. The ship's still there, though they do say a landslide buried it last winter. None of the crew returned to it once they had visited Swettenham.'

'Keith doesn't want to hear your past history,' Menderstone said, using Anderson's first name contemptuously.

'What happened to the crew?' Anderson asked.

She laughed harshly.

'They got wrapped up in your friend Arlblaster's way of life, shall we say. They became converted. . . . All except me. And since I couldn't manage the ship by myself, I also had to stay here.'

'How lucky for me, dear,' said Menderstone with heavy mock-tenderness. 'You're just my match, aren't you?'

Alice jumped up, sudden tears in her eyes.

'Shut up, you – toad! You're a pain in the neck to me and yourself and everyone! You needn't remind me what a bitch you've turned me into!' Flinging down her fork, she turned and ran from the room.

'The divine eternal female! Shall we divide what she has left of her supper between us? Menderstone asked, reaching out for Alice's plate.

Anderson stood up.

'What she said was an understatement, judging by the little I've seen here.'

'Do you imagine I enjoy this life? Or her? Or you, for that matter? Sit down, Anderson – existence is something to be got through the best way possible, isn't it? You weary me with your trite and predictable responses.'

This stormy personal atmosphere prevailed till bedtime. A bitter three-cornered silence was maintained until

Menderstone had locked Anderson into a distant part of the long building.

He had blankets with him, which he spread over the mouldy camp bed provided. He did not investigate the rooms adjoining his; several of their doors bore names vaguely familiar to him; they had been used when the intellectual group was flourishing, but were now deserted.

Tired though Anderson was, directly his head was down he began to worry about Kay and the general situation. Could his sister possibly have had any reason for returning on foot to the ship? Tomorrow, he must go and see. He turned over restlessly.

Something was watching him through the window.

In a flash, Anderson was out of bed, gripping the revolver, his heart hammering. The darkness outside was almost total. He glimpsed only a brutal silhouette in which eyes gleamed, and then it was gone.

He saw his foolishness in accepting Alice's *laissez-faire* advice to wait until Kay's captors got in touch with him. He must have been crazy to agree: or else the general lassitude of Nehru II had overcome him. Whatever was happening here, it was nasty enough to endanger Kay's life, without any messenger boys arriving first to parley about it.

Alice had said that Arlblaster lived across the river. If he were as much the key to the mystery as he seemed to be, then Arlblaster should be confronted as soon as possible. Thoroughly roused, angry, vexed with himself, Anderson went over to the window and opened it.

He peered into the scruffy night.

He could see nobody. As his eyes adjusted to the dark, Anderson discerned nearby features well enough. A bright star in the sky which he took to be Bose, Nehru II's little moon, lent some light. Swinging his leg over the sill, Anderson dropped to the ground and stood tensely outside.

Nothing moved. A dog howled. Making his way between the outer circle of houses, gun in hand, Anderson came to the river's edge. A sense of the recklessness of what he was doing assailed him, but he pressed on.

Pausing now and again to ensure he was not being followed, he moved along the river bank, avoiding the obstacles with which it was littered. He reached a bridge of a sort. A tall tree had been felled so that it lay across the stretch of water. Its underside was lapped by the river.

Anderson tucked his gun away and crossed the crude bridge with his arms outstretched for balance.

On the far side, crude attempts to cultivate the ground had been made. The untidy patchwork stopped as the upward slope of the land became more pronounced. No dwellings were visible. He stopped again and listened.

He could hear a faint and indescribable choric noise ahead. As he went forward, the noise became more distinct, less a part of the ill-defined background of furtive earth and river sounds. On the higher ground, a patch of light was now vaguely distinguishable.

This light increased as did the sound. Circumnavigating a thorny mass of brush, Anderson could see that there was a depression ahead of him in the rising valley slope. Something – a ceremony? – was going on in the depression. He ran the last few yards, doubled up, his revolver ready again, scowling in his excitement.

On the lip of the depression, he flung himself flat and peered down into the dip.

A fire was burning in the middle of the circular hollow. Round it some three dozen figures paraded, ringing two men. One of the two was a menial, throwing powder into the blaze, so that green and crimson flames spurted up; the other filled some sort of priestly role. All the others were naked. He wore a cloak and pointed hat.

He sang and waved his arms, a tall figure that woke in Anderson untraceable memories. The dancers – if their rhythmic shuffle might be called a dance – responded with low cries. The total effect, if not beautiful, was oddly moving.

Hypnotised, Anderson watched. He found that his head

was nodding in time to the chant. There was no sign of Kay here, as he had half-anticipated. But by his carrot-coloured beard and his prominent nose the priest was distinguishable even in the uncertain fire light. It was Frank Arlblaster.

Or it had been Frank Arlblaster. Items that most easily identify a man to his friends are his stance and his walk. Arlblaster's had changed. He seemed to sag at the knees and shuffle now, his torso no longer vertical to the ground. Yet the high timbre of his voice remained unaltered, though he called out in a language unknown to Anderson.

The dancers shuffled eagerly, clapping their hands, nodding their shaggy heads. Gradually it dawned on Anderson what they looked like. Beyond doubt they were the inhabitants of Swettenham. They were also, unmistakably, pre-homo sapiens. He might have been witnessing a ritual of Neanderthal men.

Mingled repulsion and elation rooted Anderson to the spot where he lay. Yes, unarguably the faces of Ell and his friends earlier had borne the touch of Neanderthal. Once the idea took, he could not shake it off.

He lay in a trance of wonder until the dance had stopped. Now all the company turned to face the spot where he lay concealed. Anderson felt the nerves tingle along his spinal cord. Arlblaster lifted an arm and pointed towards him. Then in a loud voice he cried out, the crowd shouting with him in chorus.

'Aigh murg eg neggy oggy Kay bat doo!'

The words were for Anderson.

They were unintelligible to him, yet they seemed to penetrate him. That his whereabouts was known meant nothing beside an even greater pressure on his brain. His whole being trembled on the threshold of some great disastrous revelation.

A magical trance had snared him. He was literally not himself. The meaningless words seemed to shake him to his soul. Gasping, he climbed to his feet and took himself off at a run. There was no pursuit.

He had no memory of getting back to Menderstone's place, no recollection of crossing the rough bridge, no recollection of tumbling through the window. He lay panting on the bed, his face buried in the pillow.

This state in its turn was succeeded by a vast unease. He could not sleep. Sleep was beyond him. He trembled in every limb. The hours of night dragged on for ever.

At last Anderson sat up. A faint dawn washed into the world. Taking a torch from his kit, he went to investigate the other empty rooms next to his.

A dusty corridor led to them.

Alice had said that this had been the HQ of Swettenham's original intellectual coterie. There was a library in one room, with racked spools gathering dust; Anderson did not trouble to read any titles. He felt vague antipathy for the silent ranks of them. Another room was a small committee chamber. Maps hung on the walls, meaningless, unused. He saw without curiosity that the flags stuck to one map had mostly fallen on the floor.

A third room was a recreation room. It held a curious assortment of egghead toys. There was even a model electric railway of the type fashionable on Earth a couple of centuries ago. A lathe in the corner suggested that rail and rolling stock might have been made on the premises.

Anderson peered at the track. It gleamed in his torchlight. No dust on it. He hesitatingly ran a finger along it.

A length of siding raised itself like a snake's head. Coiling up, it wrapped round Anderson's wrist, snapped tight. He pulled at it, yelling in surprise. The whole layout reared up, struggling to get at him.

He backed away, beating at the stuff as it rolled up from the table. The track writhed and launched itself at him, scattering waggons and locomotives. He fired his revolver wildly. Loops of railroad fell over him, over his head, wrapping itself madly about him.

Anderson fell to the floor, dropping his gun, dropping

30

the torch, tearing at the thin bands of metal as they bit tighter. The track threshed savagely, binding his legs together. He was shouting incoherently.

As he struggled, Menderstone ran into the room, rifle in hand, Alice behind him. It was the last thing Anderson saw as he lost consciousness.

When he roused, it was to find himself in Menderstone's living-room, sprawled on a bunk. Alice sat by him, turning towards him as he stirred. Menderstone was not in the room.

'My God . . . ' Anderson groaned. His brain felt curiously lucid, as if a fever had just left him.

'It's time you woke up. I'll get you some soup if you can manage it,' Alice said.

'Wait, Alice. Alice , . ' His lips trembled as he formed the words. 'I'm myself again. What came over me? Yesterday – I don't have a sister called Kay. I don't have a sister at all! I was an only child!'

She was unsurprised. He sat up, glaring at her.

'I guessed as much, said so to Stanley. When you brought your kit in from the vehicle there was nothing female among it.'

'My mind! I was so sure. . . . I could have pictured her, described her. . . She was actual! And yet if anyone – if you'd challenged me direct, I believe I'd have known it was an – an illusion.'

His sense of loss was forced aside as another realisation crowded in on him.

He sank down confusedly, closing his eyes, muttering. *'Aigh murg eg neggy oggy Kay bat doo.* . . . That's what they told me on the hillside: "You have no sister called Kay." That's what it meant. . . . Alice. It's so strange. . . . '

His hand sought hers and found it. It was ice cold.

'Your initial is K, Keith,' she said, pale at the lips. 'You were out there seeking yourself.'

Her face looking down at him was scared and ugly; yet a kind of gentle patience in it dissolved the ugliness.

'I'm – I'm some sort of mad,' he whispered.

'Of course you're mad!' Menderstone said, as he burst open the door. 'Let go of his hand, Alice – this is our beloved home, not the cheap seats in the feelies on Earth. Anderson, if you aren't insane, why were you rolling about on the floor, foaming at the mouth and firing your damned gun, at six o'clock this morning?'

Anderson sat up.

'You saw me entangled in that jinxed railroad when you found me, Menderstone! Another minute and it would have squeezed the life out of me.'

Menderstone looked genuinely puzzled. It was the first time Anderson had seen him without the armour of his self-assurance.

'The model railroad?' he said. 'It was undisturbed. You hadn't touched it.'

'It touched me,' Anderson said chokingly. 'It – it attacked me, wrapped itself round me like an octopus. You must have peeled it off me before getting me through here.'

'I see,' Menderstone said, his face grim.

He nodded slowly, sitting down absent-mindedly, and then nodding again to Alice.

'You see what this means, woman? Anderson's N-factor is rising to dominance. This young man is not on our side, as I suspected from the first. He's no Crow. Anderson, your time's up here, sorry! From now on, you're one of Arlblaster's men. You'll never get back to Earth.'

'On the contrary, I'm on my way back now.'

Menderstone shook his head.

'You don't know your own mind. I mean the words literally. You're doomed to stay here, playing out the miserable Life of an Ape! Earth has lost another of her estimable nonentities.'

'Menderstone, you're eaten up with hatred! You hate this planet, you hate Earth!'

Menderstone stood up again, putting his rifle down on

the table and coming across to Anderson with his fists
bunched.

'Does that make me crazy, you nincompoop? Let me
give you a good hard fact-reason why I loathe what's happening on Earth! I loathe mankind's insatiable locust-
activities, which it has the impertinence to call "assuming
mastery over nature". It has over-eaten and over-populated itself until the only other animals left are in the sea,
in zoos, or in food-factories. Now it is exhausting the fossil
fuels on which its much-vaunted technology relies. The
final collapse is due! So much for mastery of nature!
Why, it can't even master its own mind!'

'The situation may be desperate, but World Government is slowly introducing economies which –'

'World Government! You dare mention World Government? A pack of computers and automata? Isn't it an
admission that man is a locust without self-discipline that
he has to hand over control piecemeal to robots?

'And what does it all signify? Why, that civilisation is
afraid of itself, because it always tries to destroy itself.

'Why should it try to do that? Every wise man in history has asked himself why. None of them found the
answer until your pal Arlblaster tumbled on it, because
they were all looking in the wrong direction. So the
answer lies hidden here where nobody on Earth can get at
it, because no one who arrives here goes back. I could go
back, but I don't because I prefer to think of them stewing
in their own juice, in the mess they created.'

'I'm going back.' Anderson said. 'I'm going to collect
Arlblaster and I'm going back right away – when your
speech is finished.'

Menderstone laughed.

'Like to bet on it? But don't interrupt when I'm talking,
K. D. Anderson! Listen to the truth while you have the
chance, before it dies for ever.'

'Stop bellowing, Stanley!' Alice exclaimed.

'Silence, female! Attend! Do you need proof that fear-
ridden autocrats rule Earth? They have a star-drive on

their hands, they discover a dozen habitable planets within reach: what do they do? They keep them uninhabited. Having read just enough history to frighten them, they figure that if they establish colonies those colonies will rebel against them.

'Swettenham was an exceptional man. How he pulled enough strings to get us established here, I'll never know. But this little settlement – far too small to make a real colony – was an exception to point to a rule: that the ruling régime is pathologically anti-life – and must be increasingly so as robots take over.'

Anderson stood up, steadying himself against the bunk.

'Why don't you shut up, you lonely man? I'm getting out of here.'

Menderstone's reaction was unexpected. Smiling, he produced Anderson's gun.

'Suit yourself, lad! Here's your revolver. Pick it up and go.'

He dropped the revolver at his feet. Anderson stooped to pick it up. The short barrel gleamed dully. Suddenly it looked – alien, terrifying. He straightened, baffled, leaving the weapon on the floor. He moved a step away from it, his backbone tingling.

Sympathy and pain crossed Alice's face as she saw his expression. Even Menderstone relaxed.

'You won't need a gun where you're going,' he said. 'Sorry it turned out this way, Anderson! The long and tedious powers of evolution force us to be antagonists. I felt it the moment I saw you.'

'Get lost!'

Relief surged through Anderson as he emerged into the shabby sunshine. The house had seemed like a trap. He stood relaxedly in the middle of the square, sagging slightly at the knees, letting the warmth soak into him. Other people passed in ones or twos. A couple of strangely adult-looking children stared at him.

Anderson felt none of the hostility he had imagined yesterday. After all, he told himself, these folk never saw a stranger from one year to the next; to crowd round him was natural. No one had offered him harm – even Ell had a right to act to protect himself when a stranger charged round a rock carrying a gun. And when his presence had been divined on the hillside last night, they had offered him nothing more painful than revelation: 'You have no sister called Kay.'

He started walking. He knew he needed a lot of explanations; he even grasped that he was in the middle of an obscure process which had still to be worked out. But at present he was content just to exist, to *be* and not to think.

Vaguely, the idea that he must see Arlblaster stayed with him.

But new – or very ancient? – parts of his brain seemed to be in bud. The landscape about him grew in vividness, showering him with sensory data. Even the dust had a novel sweet scent.

He crossed the tree-trunk bridge without effort, and walked along the other bank of the river, enjoying the flow of the water. A few women picked idly at vegetable plots. Anderson stopped to question one of them.

'Can you tell me where I'll find Frank Arlblaster?'

'That man sleeps now. Sun go, he wakes. Then you meet him.'

'Thanks.' It was simple, wasn't it?

He walked on. There was time enough for everything. He walked a long way, steadily uphill. There was a secret about time – he had it somewhere at the back of his head – something about not chopping it into minutes and seconds. He was all alone by the meandering river now, beyond people; what did the river know of time?

Anderson noticed the watch strapped on his wrist. What did it want with him, or he with it? A watch was the badge of servitude of a time-serving culture. With sudden revulsion for it, he unbuckled it and tossed it into the river.

The shattered reflection in the water was of piled

cloud. It would rain. He stood rooted, as if casting away his watch left him naked and defenceless. It grew cold. *Something had altered. . . .* Fear came in like a distant flute.

He looked round, bewildered. A curious double noise filled the air, a low and grating rumble punctuated by high-pitched cracking sounds. Uncertain where this growing uproar came from, Anderson ran forward, then paused again.

Peering back, he could see the women still stooped over their plots. They looked tiny and crystal-clear, figures glimpsed through the wrong end of a telescope. From their indifference, they might not have heard the sound. Anderson turned round again.

Something was coming down the valley!

Whatever it was, its solid front scooped up the river and ran with it high up the hills skirting the valley. It came fast, squealing and rumbling.

It glittered like water. Yet it was not water; its bow was too sharp, too unyielding. It was a glacier.

Anderson fell to the ground.

'I'm mad, still mad!' he cried, hiding his eyes, fighting with himself to hold the conviction that this was merely a delusion. He told himself no glacier ever moved at that crazy rate – yet even as he tried to reassure himself the ground shook under him.

Groaning, he heaved himself up. The wall of ice was bearing down on him fast. It splintered and fell as it came, sending up a shower of ice particles as it was ground down, but always there was more behind it. It stretched right up the valley, grey and uncompromising, scouring out the hills' sides as it came.

Now its noise was tremendous. Cracks played over its towering face like lightning. Thunder was on its brow.

Impelled by panic, Anderson turned to run, his furs flapping against his legs.

The glacier moved too fast. It came with such force that he felt his body vibrate. He was being overtaken.

He cried aloud to the god of the glacier, remembering the old words.

There was a cave up the valley slope. He ran like mad for it, driving himself, while the ice seemed to crash and scream at his heels. With a final desperate burst of strength, he flung himself gasping through the low, dark opening, and clawed his way hand-over-fist towards the back of the cave.

He just made it. The express glacier ground on, flinging earth into the opening. For a moment the cave lit with a green-blue light. Then it was sealed up with reverberating blackness.

Sounds of rain and of his own sobbing. These were the first things he knew. Then he became aware that someone was soothing his hair and whispering comfort to him. Propping himself on one elbow, Anderson opened his eyes.

The cave entrance was unblocked. He could see grass and a strip of river outside. Rain fell heavily. His head had been resting in Alice's lap; she it was who stroked his hair. He recalled her distasteful remark about Jocasta, but this was drowned in a welter of other recollections.

'The glacier. . . . Has it gone? Where is it?'

'You're all right, Keith. There's no glacier round here. Take it easy!'

'It came bursting down the valley towards me. . . . Alice, how did you get here?'

She put out a hand to pull his head down again, but he evaded it.

'When Stanley turned you out, I couldn't bear to let you go like that, friendless, so I followed you. Stanley was furious, of course, but I knew you were in danger. Look, I've brought your revolver.'

'I don't want it! – It's haunted. . . . '

'Don't say that, Keith. Don't turn into a Neanderthal!'

'What?' He sat fully upright, glaring at her through the gloom. 'What the hell do you mean?'

'You know. You understand, don't you?'

'I don't understand one bit of what's going on here. You'd better start explaining – and first of all, I want to know what it looked as if I was doing when I ran into this cave.'

'Don't get excited, Keith. I'll tell you what I can.' She put her hand over his before continuing. 'After you'd thrown your watch into the river, you twisted and ran about a bit – as if you were dodging something – and then rushed into here.'

'You didn't *hear* anything odd? See anything?'

'No.'

'And no glaciers?'

'Not on Nehru, no!'

'And was I – dressed in skins?'

'Of course you weren't!'

'My mind. . . . I'd have sworn there was a glacier. . . . Moving too fast . . .'

Alice's face was pale as she shook her head.

'Oh, Keith, you are in danger. You must get back to Earth at once. Can't you see this means you have a Neanderthal layer in your brain? Obviously you were experiencing a race memory from that newly opened layer. It was so strong it took you over entirely for a while. You *must* get away.'

He stood up, his shoulders stooped to keep his skull from scraping the rock overhead. Rain drummed down outside. He shook with impatience.

'Alice, Alice, begin at the beginning, will you? I don't know a thing except that I'm no longer in control of my own brain.'

'Were you ever in control? Is the average person? Aren't all the sciences of the mind attempts to bring the uncontrollable under control? Even when you're asleep, it's only the neo-cortex switched off. The older limbic layers – they never sleep. There's no day or night, that deep.'

38

'So what? What has the unconscious to do with this particular set-up?'

' "The unconscious" is a pseudo-scientific term to cover a lack of knowledge. You have a moron in your skull who never sleeps, sweetie! He gives you a nudge from time to time; it's crazy thoughts you overhear when you think you're dreaming.'

'Look, Alice –'

She stood up too. Anxiety twisted her face.

'You wanted an explanation, Keith. Have the grace to listen to it. Let me start from the other end of the tale, and see if you like it any better.

'Neanderthal was a species of man living in Europe some eighty thousand and more years ago, before homo sap came along. They were gentle creatures, close to nature, needing few artefacts, brain cases bigger even than homo sap. They were peaceful, unscientific in a special sense you'll understand later.

'Then along came a different species, the Crows – Cro-Magnons, you'd call them – Western man's true precursors. Being warlike, they defeated the Neanderthals at every encounter. They killed off the men and mated with the Neanderthal women, which they kept captive. We, modern man, sprang from the bastard race so formed. This is where Arlblaster's theory comes in.

'The mixture never quite mixed. That's why we still have different, often antagonistic, blood groups today – and why there are inadequate neural linkages in the brain. Crow and Neanderthal brains never established full contact. Crow was dominant, but a power-deprived lode of Neanderthal lingered on, as apparently vestigial as an appendix.'

'My God, I'd like a mescahale.' Anderson said. They had both sat down again, ignoring the occasional beads of moisture which dripped down their necks from the roof of the cave. Alice was close to him, her eyes bright in the shadow.

'Do you begin to see it historically, Keith? Western

39

man with this clashing double heritage in him has always been restless. Freud's theory of the id comes near to labelling the Neanderthal survivor in us. Arthur Koestler also came close. All civilisation can be interpreted as a Crow attempt to vanquish that survivor, and to escape from the irrational it represents – yet at the same time the alien layer is a rich source for all artists, dreamers, and creators: because it is the very well of magic.

'The Neanderthal had magic powers. He lived in a dawn age, the dawn of rationality, when it's no paradox to say that supernatural and natural are one. The Crows, our ancestors, were scientific, or potentially scientific – spear-makers, rather than fruit-gatherers. They had a belief, fluctuating at first maybe, in cause and effect. As you know, all Western science represents a structure built on our acceptance of unalterable cause and effect.

'Such belief is entirely alien to the Neanderthal. He knows only happening, and from this stems his structure of magic. I use the present tense because the Neanderthal is still strong in man – and, on Nehru II, he is not only strong but free, liberated at last from his captor, the Crow.'

Anderson stirred, rubbing his wet skull.

'I suppose you're right '

'There's proof enough here,' she said bitterly.

'I suppose it does explain why the civilisation of old Europe – the ancient battle-ground of Cro-Magnon and Neanderthal – and the civilisations that arose from it in North America are the most diverse and most turbulent ever know. But this brings us back to Arlblaster, doesn't it? I can see that what has happened in Swettenham connects logically with his theory. The Brittany skull he found back in the eighties was pure Neanderthal, yet only a few hundred years old. Obviously it belonged to a rare throwback.'

'But how rare? You could pass a properly dressed Neanderthal in the streets of New York and never give him a second glance. Stanley says you often do.'

'Let's forget Stanley! Arlblaster followed up his theory. . . . Yes, I can see it myself. The proportion of Neanderthal would presumably vary from person to person. I can run over my friends mentally now and guess in which of them the proportion is highest.'

'Exactly.' She smiled at him, reassured and calmer now, even as he was, as she nursed his hand and his revolver. 'And because the political economic situation on Earth is as it is, Arlblaster found a way here to develop his theory and turn it into practice – that is, to release the prisoner in the brain. Earth would allow Swettenham's group little in the way of machinery or resources in its determination to keep them harmless, so they were thrust close to nature. That an intellectual recognition brought the Neanderthal to the surface, freed it.'

'Everyone turned Neanderthal, you mean?'

'Here on Nehru, which resembles prehistoric Earth in some respects, the Neanderthal represents better survival value than Crow. Yet not everyone transformed, no. Stanley Menderstone did not. Nor Swettenham. Nor several others of the intellectuals. Their N-factor, as Stanley calls it, was either too low or non-existent.'

'What happened to Swettenham?'

'He was killed. So were the other pure Crows, all but Stanley, who's tough – as you saw. There was a heap of trouble at first, until they fully understood the problem and sorted themselves out.'

'And these two patrol ships World Government sent?'

'I saw what happened to the one that brought me. About seventy-five per cent of the crew had a high enough N-factor to make the change; a willingness to desert helped them. The others . . . died out. Got killed, to be honest. All but me. Stanley took care of me.'

She laughed harshly. 'If you can call it care.

'I've had my belly full of Stanley and Nehru II, Keith. I want you to take me back with you to Earth.'

Anderson looked at her, still full of doubt.

'What about my N-factor? Obviously I've got it in me.

41

Hence the glacier, which was a much stronger danger signal from my brain than the earlier illusion about having a sister. Hence, I suppose, my new fears of manufactured Crow objects like watches, revolvers and . . . model railroads. Am I Crow or not, for heaven's sake?'

'By the struggle you've been through with yourself, I'd say that you're equally balanced. Perhaps you can even decide. Which do you want to be?'

He looked at her in amazement.

'Crow, of course: my normal self – who'd become a shambling, low-browed, shaggy tramp by choice?'

'The adjectives you use are subjective and not really terms of abuse – in fact, they're Crow propaganda. Or so a Neanderthal would say. The two points of view are irreconcilable.'

'Are you seriously suggesting . . . Alice, they're submen!'

'To us they appear so. Yet they have contentment, and communion with the forces of Earth, and their magic. Nor are their brains inferior to Crow brains.'

'Much good it did them! The Cro-Magnons still beat them.'

'In a sense they have not yet been beaten. But their magic needs preparation, incantation – it's something they can't do while fending off a fusillade of arrows. But left to themselves they can become spirits, animals – '

'Wooly rhinoceroses for instance?'

'Yes.'

'To lure me from my wheeled machine, which they would fear! My God, Alice, can it be true . . . ' He clutched his head and groaned, then looked up to enquire, 'Why are you forcing their point of view on me, when you're a Crow?'

'Don't you see, my dear?' Her eyes were large as they searched his. 'To find how strong your N-factor is. To find if you're friend or enemy. When this rain stops, I *must* go back. Stanley will be looking for *me*, and it wouldn't surprise me if Arlblaster were not looking for you; he must know you've had time to sort things out in your mind. So I want to know if I can come back to Earth with you. . . . '

He shook himself, dashed a water drip off his forehead, tried to delay giving an answer.

'Earth's not so bad,' he said. 'Menderstone's right, of course; it is regimented – it would never suit an individualist like him. It's not so pretty as Nehru. . . . Yes, Alice, I'll take you back if you want to come. I can't leave you here.'

She flung herself on to him, clasping him in her arms, kissing his ear and cheek and lips.

'I'm a loving woman,' she whispered fiercely. 'As even Stanley – '

They stiffened at a noise outside the cave, audible above the rain. Anderson turned his head to look where she was looking. Rain was falling more gently now. Before its fading curtain a face appeared.

The chief features of this face were its low brow, two large and lustrous eyes, a prominent nose, and a straggling length of wet, sandy beard. It was Frank Arlblaster.

He raised both hands.

'Come to see me, child of Earth, as I come to see you, peaceful, patient, all-potent – '

As more of him rose into view in the cave mouth, Alice fired the revolver. The bellow of its report in the confined space was deafening. At ten yards' range, she did not miss. Arlblaster clutched at his chest and tumbled forward into the wet ground, crying inarticulately.

Anderson turned on Alice, and struck the gun from her hand.

'Murder, sheer murder! You shouldn't have done it! You shouldn't have done – '

She smacked him across the cheek.

'If you're Crow, he's your enemy as well as mine! He'd have killed me! He's an Ape. . . . ' She drew a long shuddering breath. 'And now we've got to move fast for your ship before the pack hunts us down.'

'You make me sick!' He tried to pick up the revolver

43

but could not bring himself to touch it.

'Keith, I'll make it up to you on the journey home, I promise. I – I was desperate!'

'Just don't talk to me! Come on, let's git.'

They slid past Arlblaster's body, out into the mizzling rain. As they started down the slope, a baying cry came from their left flank. A group of Neanderthals, men and women, stood on a promontory only two hundred yards away. They must have witnessed Arlblaster's collapse and were slowly marshalling their forces. As Alice and Anderson appeared, some of the men ran forward.

'Run!' Alice shouted. 'Down to the river! Swim it and we're safe.'

Close together, they sped down the slippery incline where an imaginary glacier had flowed. Without a pause or word, they plunged through reeds and mud and dived fully dressed into the slow waters. Making good time, the Neanderthals rushed down the slope after them, but halted when they reached the river.

Gaining the far bank, Anderson turned and helped Alice out of the water. She collapsed puffing on the grass.

'Not so young as I was. . . . We're safe now, Keith. Nothing short of a forest fire induces those apes to swim. But we still might meet trouble this side. . . . We'll avoid the settlement. Even if the apes there aren't after us, we don't want to face Stanley with his rifle. . . . Poor old Stanley! Give me a hand up. . . . '

Anderson moved on in surly silence. His mind was troubled by Arlblaster's death; and he felt he was being used.

The rain ceased as they pressed forward among dripping bush. Travelling in a wide arc, they circled the village and picked up a track which led back towards Anderson's ship.

Alice grumbled intermittently as they went. At last Anderson turned on her.

'You don't have to come with me, Alice. If you want to go back to Stanley Menderstone!'

44

'At least he cared about a woman's feelings.'

'I warn you that they are not so fussy on Earth, where women don't have the same scarcity value.' He hated himself for speaking so roughly. He needed solitude to sort out the turmoil in his brain.

Alice plodded along beside him without speaking. Sun gleamed. At last the black hull of the ship became visible between trees.

'You'll have to work on Earth!' he taunted her. 'The robocracy will direct you.'

'I shall get married. I've still got some looks.'

'You've forgotten something, honey. Women have to have work certificates before they can marry these days. Regimentation will do you good.'

A wave of hatred overcame him. He remembered the priestly Arlblaster dying. When Alice started to snap back at him, Anderson struck her on the shoulder. A look of panic and understanding passed over her face.

'Oh, Keith . . .' she said. 'You . . .' Her voice died; a change came over her face. He saw her despair before she turned and was running away, back towards the settlement, calling inarticulately as she ran.

Anderson watched her go. Then he turned and sidled through the dripping trees. At last – free! Himself! She was a Crow squaw.

His ship no longer looked welcoming. He splashed through a puddle and touched it, withdrawing his hand quickly. Distorted by the curve of the hull, his reflection peered at him from the polished metal. He did not recognise himself.

'Someone there imprisoned in Crow ship,' he said, turning away.

The breath of the planet was warm along his innocent cheek. He stripped off his damp clothes and faded among the leaves and uncountable grasses and the scents of soil and vegetation. Shadow and light slithered over his skin in an almost tangible pattern before foliage embraced him and he was lost entirely into his new Eden.

45

The proud author lay where he was on the floor of the small room, among the metal sheets he had worn as camouflage while hiding with the humots. Since the Tenth Dominant finished reading his story – that poor thing written before he had wisdom – silence lay between the Dominant and the Chief Scanner; though whether or not they were communicating by UHF, Anderson could not tell.

He decided he had better do something. Sitting up, he said, 'How about letting me go free? . . . Or how about letting me go back to the zoo? . . . Well, at least take me into a room that's big enough for me.'

The Dominant spoke. 'We need to ask you questions about your story. Is it true or not true?'

'It's fiction. Lousy or otherwise, it exists in its own right.'

'Some things in it are true – you are. So is or was Frank Arlblaster. So is or was Stanley Menderstone. But other things are false. You did not stay always on Nehru II. You came back to Earth.'

'The story is a fiction. Forget it! It has nothing to do with you. Or with me, now. I only write poetry now – that story is just a thing I wrote to amuse myself.'

'We do not understand it. You must explain it.'

'Oh, Christ! . . . Look, I wouldn't bother about it! I wrote it on the journey back to Earth from Nehru II, just to keep myself amused. When I got here, it was to find the various surviving Master Boffs were picking up such bits of civilisation as were left round the world after Nuclear Week! The story immediately became irrelevant.'

'We know all about Nuclear Week. We do not know about your story. We insist that we know about it.'

As Anderson sighed, he nevertheless recognised that more must lie in the balance here than he understood.

'I've been a bad boy, Dominant, I know. I escaped from the zoo. Put me back there, let me settle back with my wife; for my part, I'll not attempt to escape again. *Then* we'll talk about my story.'

The silence lasted only a fraction of a second. 'Done,' said the Dominant, with splendid mastery of humanic idiom.

The zoo was not unpleasant. By current standards, it was vast, and the flats in the new human-type skyscrapers not too cramped; the liberals admitted that the Hive had been generous about space. There were about twenty thousand people here, the East Coast survivors of Nuclear Week. The robocracy had charge of them; they, in their turn, had charge of all the surviving wild life that the automata could capture. Incongruous among the tall flat-blocks stood cages of exotic animals collected from shattered zoos – a pride of lions, some leopards, several cheetahs, an ocelot, camels. There were monkey houses, ostrich houses, elephant houses, aquaria, reptilia. There were pens full of pigs and sheep and cows. Exotic and native birds were captive in aviaries.

Keith Anderson sat on the balcony of his flat with his wife, Sheila, and drank an ersatz coffee, looking out on to the pens below, not without relish.

'Well, the robots are behaving very strangely,' Sheila was saying. 'When you disappeared, three of the very tiny ones came and searched everywhere. Your story was the only thing they seemed interested in. They must have photostatted it.'

'I remember now – it was in the trunk under the bed. I'd forgotten all about it till they mentioned it – my sole claim to literary fame!'

'But that side of it can't interest them. What are they excited about?'

He looked amusedly at her. She was still partly a stranger to him, though a beloved one. In the chaos to which he returned after the Nehru trip, it was a case of marrying any eligible girl while they were available – men outnumbered women two to one; he'd been lucky in his blind choice. Sheila might not be particularly beauti-

47

ful, but she was good in bed, trustworthy, and intelligent. You could ask for no more.

He said, 'Do you ever admit the truth of the situation to yourself, Sheila? The new automats are now the superior race. They have a dozen faculties to each one of ours. They're virtually indestructible. Small size is clearly as much an enormous advantage to them as it would be a disadvantage to us. We've heard rumours that they were on the threshold of some staggering new discovery – from what I overheard the Tenth Dominant say, they are on the brink of moving into some staggering new dimensions of which we can probably never even get a glimpse. And yet – '

'And yet they need your story!' She laughed – sympathetically, so that he laughed with her.

'Right! They need my goddamned story! Listen – their powers of planning and extrapolation are proved miraculous. But they cannot *imagine*; imagination might even be an impediment for them. So the Dominant, who can tap more knowledge than you or I dream of is baffled by a work of fiction. He needs my imagination.'

'Not entirely, Mr Anderson.'

Anderson jumped up, cup in hand, as his wife gave a small scream.

Perched on the balcony rail, enormously solid-looking, yet only six inches high, was the stubby shape of an automaton!

Furious, Anderson flung his cup, the only weapon to hand. It hit the machine four-square, shattered, and fell away. The machine did not even bother to refer to the matter.

'We understand imagination. We wish to ask you more questions about the background to your story.'

Anderson sat down, took Sheila's hand, and made an anatomical suggestion which no automaton could have carried out.

'We want to ask you more questions about the story.

Why did you write that you stayed on Nehru when really you came back?'

'Are you the Chief Scanner who captured me on D-Dump?'

'You are speaking with Tenth Dominant, in command of Eastern Seaboard. I have currently taken over Chief Scanner for convenience of speaking with you.'

'Sort of mechanical transvestism, eh?'

'Why did you write that you stayed when you in reality came back?'

'You'd better give him straight answers, Keith,' Sheila said.

He turned to her irritably, 'How do I know the answer? It was just a story! I suppose it made a better ending to have the Anderson-figure stay on Nehru. There was this Cro-Magnon-Neanderthal business in the story, and I made myself out to be more Neanderthal than Crow for dramatic effect. Just a lot of nonsense really?'

'Why do you call it nonsense when you wrote it yourself?' asked the Dominant. It had settled in the middle of the coffee-table now.

The man sighed wearily. 'Because I'm older now. The story was a lot of nonsense because I injected this Crow-Neanderthal theory, which is a bit of free-wheeling young man tripe. It just went in to try to explain what actually happened on Nehru – how the egghead camp broke down and everything. The theory doesn't hold water for a moment; I see that now, in the light of what happened since, Nuclear Week and all that. You see – '

He stopped. He stopped in mid-sentence and stared at the little complex artifact confronting him. It was speaking to him but he did not hear, following his own racing thoughts. He stretched forward his hand and picked it up; the automaton was heavy and warm, only mildly frightening, slightly, slightly vibrating at the power of its own voice; the Dominant did not stop him picking it up. He stared at it as if he had never seen such a thing before.

'I repeat, how would you revise your theory now?' said the automaton.

Anderson came back to reality.

'Why should I help you? To your kind, man is just another animal in a zoo, a lower species.'

'Not so. We revere you as ancestors, and have never treated you otherwise.'

'Maybe. Perhaps we regard animals in somewhat the same way since, even in the darkest days of over-population and famine, we strove to stock our zoos in ever-greater numbers. So perhaps I will tell you my current theory. . . . It is real theory now; in my story that theory was not worth the name – it was a stunt, an intellectual high-jink, a bit of science fiction. Now I have lived and thought and loved and suffered, and I have talked to other men. So if I tell you the theory now, you will know it is worked for – part of the heritage of all men in this zoo.'

'This time it is truth not false?'

'You are the boss – *you* must decide that. There are certainly two distinct parts of the brain, the old limbic section and the neo-cortex surrounding it, the bit that turns a primate into a man. That much of my story was true. There's also a yet older section, but we won't complicate the picture. Roughly speaking, the limbic is the seat of the emotions, and the neo-cortex the seat of the intelligence. Okay. In a crisis, the new brain is still apt to cut out and the old brain take over.

'And that in a nutshell is why mankind never made the grade. We are a failed species. We never got away from the old animal inheritance. We could never become the distinct species we should have been.'

'Oh, darling, it's not as bad as that –'

He squeezed Sheila's hand. 'You girls are always optimists.' He winked the eye the Dominant could not see.

The Dominant said, 'How does this apply to what happened on Nehru II?'

'My story departed – not from the facts but from the correct explanation of the facts. The instinct to go there on Swettenham's part was sound. He and Arlblaster and the rest believed that on a planet away from animals, mankind could achieve its true stature – homo superior, shall we say? What I called the N-factor let them down. The strain was too great, and they mainly reverted instead of evolving.'

'But you believe a species can only escape its origins by removing itself entirely from the site of those origins.'

Sheila said, 'That was the whole human impulse behind space travel – to get to worlds where it would be possible to become more human.'

The Dominant sprang from Anderson's hands and circled under the low ceiling – an oddly uneasy gesture.

'But the limbic brain – such a small part of the brain, so deep-buried!'

'The seat of the instincts.'

'The seat of the instincts. . . . Yes, and so the animal part of man brought you to disaster.'

'Does that answer all your questions?'

The automaton came back down and settled on the table. 'One further question. What do you imagine would happen to mankind now, after Nuclear Week, if he was left alone on Earth?'

Anderson had to bury his face in his hands to hide his triumph.

'I guess we'd carry on. Under D-Dump, and the other dumps, lie many of the old artefacts. We'd dig them up and carry on.'

'But Earth's resources are almost spent. That was mankind's doing, not the doing of automata.'

The man smiled. 'Maybe we'd revert, then. It is a sort of Neanderthal planet, isn't it? Things go wrong for animals and men and robots, don't they? Just as they did for dinosaurs and Neanderthals!'

'I am going now,' said the Tenth Dominant. His voice cut. He disappeared.

Gasping, Anderson clutched his wife. 'Don't say a

word! Come inside. Hold me and kiss me. Pray, if you feel like it.'

All she said as they went to their bed was, 'Maybe you will end up a writer after all. You show a talent for story-telling!'

It was all of five days before the humans in the big zoo noticed that the automata were disappearing. Suddenly, they were all gone, leaving no word. The whole conti-nent, presumably the whole world, lay almost empty; and mankind began to walk back into it on his own ill-shod feet.

'And you did it, Keith Anderson!' Sheila cried.

'Nope. They did it themselves. They made the right decision – maybe I spurred them on.'

'You did it – a genius who is now going to turn himself into a pig-breeder.'

'I happen to like pigs.' As he spoke, he stood in the middle of a dozen of the animals, which he and Sheila had taken charge of.

'So the entire automata-horde had disappeared into the invo-spectrum, wherever that is, leaving us our world. . . . '

'It's a different world. Let's try and make it saner than the old one.'

Pious hope? New Year's resolution? New design for living? He could not tell, although it filled his mind.

As they drove the pigs before them, Anderson said, 'When the Dominant got on to the subject of our animal inheritance, I remembered just in time that I heard him tell the Scanner. "We must free ourselves from our human heritage." You can see the spot they were in! They had scrapped the humots, all too closely anthropomorphic in design, and taken more functional forms themselves. But they still had to acknowledge us as father-figures, and could never escape from many human and naturalistic concepts, however much they tried, as long as they re-mained in a naturalistic setting. Now, in this unimagin-able alternative energy universe, which they have finally cracked, they can be pure automata – which is something else we can't conceive! So they become a genuine species. Pure automata. . . . '

They broke off to drive their pigs through the doorway, doubling back and forth until all the animals were inside, squealing and trying to leap over one another's backs. Anderson slammed the outer door at once, gasping.

'What I'd like to know is, what would it be like to be pure human being!' Sheila exclaimed.

He had no answer. He was thinking. Of course, they needed a dog! On D-Dump there were feral hounds, whose young could be caught and trained.

It was lucky that the ground-floor tenants had gone. Most humans had moved out of the zoo as soon as possible, so that the great block of flats was almost empty. They shut the pigs in the hall for the night and climbed up rather wearily to their flat.

Today, they were too tired to bother about the future.

RANDY'S SYNDROME

Gordana stood in the foyer of the Maternity Hospital, idly watching cubision as she waited for Sonia Greenslade. A university programme was showing shots of fleas of the cliff swallow climbing up a cliff swallow's legs, alternating with close-ups of a cadaverous professor delivering himself at length on the subject of parasitology. Gordana felt convinced that she could understand him if she tried, and if there were not weightier things on her mind.

When Sonia came up, her face crimson, she took Gordana's arm and tried to hustle her away.

'Just a moment,' Gordana said. A line of fleas was working its way steadily up a sheet of damp laboratory glass. 'Negative geotropism!'

'Let's get out of here, honey!' Sonia begged. She tugged Gordana towards the stride-strip entrance of the hospital, looking rather like a mouse towing a golden hamster – for she was only five months on the way against the blonde Gordana's nine-month season. 'Let's get home – you can watch CB in my place if you like. I just can't bear to stay here one moment longer. I was brought up modest. The things that doctor does to a woman without turning a hair! – Makes me want to die!'

The high colour disappeared from her cheeks as they sped homewards along the strip. This was the quietest time of day in their level, mid-morning, when most of the millions of the city's inhabitants were swallowed into offices and factories. For all that, the moving streets with their turntable intersections were spilling over with people, the monoducts hissed overhead, and beneath their feet they could feel and hear the snarl of the subwalk supply lanes. Both women were glad to get into Block 661.

'Maybe we'd better go into the canteen,' Sonia suggested, as they swept into the porch. 'John was on night duty last night, and he's bound to be writing now. He'll get all neurotic if we disturb him.'

Gordana just wanted to be by herself; but since she was wrapped in placidity at this period, she said nothing, allowing her voluble little friend to drag her into the bright-lit canteen on the second level. She sank gratefully into a chair, setting her bulk down into comfort with a sigh.

'He sure works hard,' Sonia said. 'He's nearly finished the eighteenth chapter.'

'Good.' Although the Greenslades happened to live in a flat on the same floor as Gordana and Randy, Gordana doubted whether they would ever have become friends but for the chance of their pregnancies coinciding. Randy was a simple guy who worked on an assembly line in the day and watched cubision and cuddled his wife in the evening; John was a scholar who packaged dinner cereals all night and wrote a book on the Effect of the Bible on Western Civilisation, 1611–2005, during the day. Gordana was large and content, Sonia was small and nervous. The more Sonia talked, the more Gordana retreated into her little world dominated by her loving husband and, increasingly, her unborn child.

Together, the two girls scanned the canteen menu. Rodent's meat was in fashion this week; the man at the next table was eating chinchilla con carne. Sonia ordered a beaver-berger. Gordana settled for a cup of coffeemix.

'Go on and eat if you want to; it's all the same to me.'
She looked round nervously. The voice sounded so terribly loud to her, a shout that filled her being, yet nobody else noticed a thing. 'Just coffeemix,' she subvocalised. Mercifully, silence then; it had gone back into

its mysterious slumbers, but she knew it would soon rouse completely and wanted to be alone with it when that happened.

'. . . Still and all, I mustn't keep on about John,' Sonia said. 'It's just – well, you know, he works such long hours and I don't get enough sleep and he will play back what he's written so loud. Some of it is very interesting, especially the bit he's got to now about the Bible and evolution. John says that even if the Bible was wrong about evolution and society, that's no reason for it to have been banned by the government in 2005, and that it doesn't have the harmful effects that they claim. . . . Say, honey, what did the medics say about you back at the hospital? Didn't they say you were overdue?'

'Yep, ten days overdue. My gynaecologist wants to induce it next week, but I'm not going to let him. Men never have any faith in nature. I want my baby born when it wants to be born and not before.'

Sonia tilted her little head to one side and fluttered her eyes in admiration 'My, you're so good at sticking up for yourself, Gordana Hicks, I just wish I were that brave. But suppose they grab you next week and *force* you to go through with it?'

'I'm not going back there next week, Sonia.'

'But I'll be lonely there without you!'

'You'll get by.'

'Oh, I'll never get by. I get just so embarrassed, it isn't true. And having to sit in that hot room with all those other girls with no panties on for half an hour, and you can guess they are all placed the same way.' She glanced anxiously at the man at the next table to see if he had heard what she said. 'Well, I just think they run that place as if it was an assembly line of breeding cows.'

'They're certainly crowded – '

'Crowded! I said to one of the other girls, I said, "They run this place as if it was an assembly line of breeding cows", and do you know what she told me – big woman with straggly hair and her breath smells of garlic – she

57

said that a million and a half babies are born every week in this city alone! So you see why – '

Gordana laughed, the mellow chime that her husband claimed would open any door. 'A million and a half babies a week! No, I don't believe it.'

'Well, perhaps it was a million and a half a year. But whatever it was, I can tell you it was a pretty high figure and this woman said the city authorities were desperate about living space and the food shortage. Wouldn't care to finish my beaver-berger, would you?'

'It's the fault of the men,' Gordana said crisply, rising to her feet. 'They got us in this condition; they should organise the world better, Instead, all they do is talk.'

'Isn't that just what I tell John,' Sonia agreed, wiping her mouth. 'He says it's the influence of the Bible still lingering on, with all its "go forth and multiply" propaganda. But men have always got excuses – the longer I live with them, really, the more I despise them. I know my mother used to say "Familiarity breeds contempt".'

'But you can't breed without it,' called the man at the next table, smiling coarsely over his plate of meat.

Offended, the two women whisked out of the canteen, though Gordana's whisk was remarkably like a lumber.

Gordana kept their flat very tidy and cleaned, or had done until the languors of this last month. Not that there was much to keep clean. She and Randy had a single room in which to live, ten feet by twelve, with a bed that swung ingeniously down from the ceiling. Their one un-opening window looked on to the hissing monoduct, so that they generally kept it opaqued.

They were six levels below ground level. Their building, a low *avant garde* one situated in the suburbs, had thirty-two stories, twenty-four of them above ground. With luck, and not too many kids, they might expect to rise, on Randy's pay-scale, to the twenty-eighth floor in successful middle age, only to sink back underground, layer by layer, year by year, like sediment, as they grew older and less able to earn. Unless something awful happened, like civilisation falling or bursting apart at the seams, as it threatened to do.

Having left Sonia at her flat door, tiptoeing in to see if John was working or sleeping, Gordana put her feet up in her own room and massaged her ankles. Listlessly, she switched on the wall taper, to listen to the daily news that had just popped through the slot.

It had nothing to offer by way of refreshment. The project for levelling the Rocky Mountains was meeting trouble; the plague of mutated fish was still climbing out of the sea near Atlantic City, covering sidewalks a foot deep; the birth rate had doubled in the last ten years, the suicide rate in the last five; Jackie 'Knees' Norris, famed CB star, was unconscious from a stroke. Abroad, there was a rash of troubles. Europe was about to blow itself up, Indonesia had done so. Gordana switched off before the catalogue was complete.

A vague claustrophobia seized her. She just wished Randy earned enough to let them live up in the daylight. She wanted her baby brought up in daylight.

'Then why doesn't Randy study for a better job?'

'Negative geotropism,' she answered aloud. 'We work our way up towards the sun like the fleas working their way up the swallow's legs.'

The foetus made no attempt to understand that, perhaps guessing that it was never likely to meet either swallows or fleas in the flesh. Instead, it repeated its question in the non-voice that roared through Gordana's being, *'Why doesn't Randy study for a better job?'*

'Do try and call him Daddy, or Pop, not Randy. It makes it sound as if I wasn't married to him for the next five years.'

'Why doesn't he try and get a better job?'

'Darling, you are about to emerge into a suffocatingly overcrowded world. There's no room for *anything* any longer, not even for success. But your dad and me are happy as things are, and I don't want him worrying. Look at that John Greenslade! He spent five years working at the CB University course, doubling up on History and Religion and Literature streams, and where'd it get him when he took his diploma? Why, nowhere – all places were filled. So he drives himself and his wife mad, working all his spare hours, trying to pump all that education back out of his system into some magnabook that nobody is going to publish. No, my boy, we're just fine as we are. You'll see as soon as you arrive!'

'*I don't want to arrive!*'

'So you keep saying – it was the first thing you ever said to me, three months ago. But nature must take its course.'

Ironically, his voice echoed hers: '*Nature must take its course.*'

He had heard her say it often enough, or listened to it echo round her thoughts since the time he had first made her aware that his intelligence was no longer dormant. Gordana had never been scared. The embryo was a part of her, its booming and soundless voice – produced, she suspected, as much in her own head as in his little cranium that was fed by her bloodstream – seemed as much part of her as the weight she carried before her.

Randy had been hostile when she told him about the conversations at first. She still wondered what he really thought, but was grateful that he seemed resigned to the situation; she wanted no trouble. Perhaps he still did not fully believe, just because he could not hear that monstrous tiny voice himself. However he had managed it, he seemed content with things as they were.

But when Randy returned that evening, he had a nasty surprise for her. She knew something was wrong the moment he came in, even before he kissed her.

'We're in trouble, old pet,' he said. He was pale, small, squat – The Packaged Modern Man, she thought, with nothing but affection – and tonight the genial look about his eyes was extinguished. 'I've notice to quit at the end of the week.'

'Oh, sweetie, why? They can't do this to you, you know

they can't! You were so good at the job, I'm sure!'

After the usual protestations, he broke off and tried to explain.

'It's this World Reallocation of Labour Act – they're closing the factory down. Everyone's been fired.'

'They can't do that!' she wailed. 'People will always need wrist-computers!'

'Sure they will, but we manufacture for the Mid-European block. Now we've set up a factory in Prague, Czechoslovakia, that is going to turn out all parts on the spot, cut distribution costs, give employment to a million Mid-Europeans.'

'What about a million Mid-Americans!'

'Hon, you think we got over-population problems, you should see Europe!'

'But we're at *war* with Czechoslovakia!'

He sighed. You couldn't explain these things to women. 'That's just a political war,' he said, 'like our contained war with Mongolia, but a degree less hot. Don't forget that the Czechs are not only in the Comblok politically, they are now in the Eurcom economically, not to mention Natforce strategically. We have to help those goddamned Czechs or bust.'

'So you're bust,' she sighed.

Randy was annoyed. 'I could have broken this news better if you could still manage to sit on my knee. When are you going to give birth, I want to know? What are they going to do about it down at that goddamned hospital?'

'Randy Hicks, I will give birth when I am good and ready and not before.'

'It's all very well for you, but how do you think a man feels? I want you with your figure back again, sweetie pie.' He sank to his knees against her, whispering, 'I want to love you again, sugar, show you how much I love you.'

'Oh no, you don't!' she exclaimed. 'We've only been married ten months yet! I know you went against the law, Randy, I'm not a fool. We're just not going to have a whole brood of kids – I want to see daylight through my window before I die – I –'

'Daylight! All you think of is daylight!'

'Tell him I won't be born until the world is a fit place to be born into!'

The sound of that bloodstream voice recalled Gordana to realities. She laughed and said, 'Randy junior says he is not appearing on the world scene until the world scene looks rosier. We'd better try to fix you up with a job, pet, instead of quarrelling.'

The days that followed were exhausting for both Gordana and Randy. Randy left the one-room flat early every morning to go looking for a job. Since private transport had long since been forbidden inside city areas, he was forced to use the crowded urban transports, often travelling miles to chase the rumour of work. Once he took a job for three days pouring concrete, where the foundations of a new government building had pierced through the earth's crust into the Mohorovičic discontinuity below, creating a subterranean volcanic eruption; then he was on the hunt again, more exhausted than ever.

Gordana was left alone. She had Sonia Greenslade to visit with her once or twice, but Sonia was too busy worrying about John to be best company: John was under threat of dismissal at the packing plant if his work did not improve. On the next day that she was due to report to the hospital, Gordana went out instead and took a robowl up to the surface.

It was a fine sweet sunlit day with one white cloud shaped like a flea moving in a south-westerly direction over the city. This was summer as she remembered it; she had forgotten how sharply the summer breeze whistled between blocks and how chill the shadows of the giant buildings were. She had forgotten, too, that it was forbidden to walk on the surface. And she had forgotten that transport was for free only on one's own living-level. She paid out of her little stock of cash to get to the first green park.

The park was encased in glass and air-conditioned against the hazards of weather. It was tiled throughout and thronged with people at this hour of the afternoon. An old church stood in the middle of the crowded place, converted into a combined museum and fun house. She went in, past the turnstiles and swings and flashing machines and 'Test-Your-Heterosexuality' girls, into a dim side arcade where vestments were exhibited. People were pressed thick against the cases, but there was space in the middle of the aisle to stand still a minute without getting jostled. Gordana stood without getting jostled and, to her surprise, began to cry.

She did it very quietly, but was unable to stop. People began to gather round her, curious at the sight. Hooliganism one noticed in public, but never crying. Soon there was a big crowd round her. The men began to laugh uncomfortably and make remarks. Two gawky creatures with shaven heads and sidewhiskers, who could not be said to be either boys or men, began to mimic her for each other's delight. The blobby-nosed one gave a running commentary on Gordana's actions.

'New tear forming up in her left eye, folks. This one'll be a beaut, that's my guess, and I've seen tears. I'm World's Champion Tear Spotter Number One! Yeah, it's swelling up to the lid, yeah, gosh, there she tumbles, very pretty, very nice, nice delivery, she's infanticipating I should say, got no husband, just a good-time girl having a bad time, and now another tear gathering strength in her right eye – no, no, tears in both eyes! Oh, this is really some performance here, and she's trying to catch them in a handkerchief, she's making quite a noise – '

'Help me!' Gordana said to her unborn child. It was the first time she had ever addressed it without waiting to hear it speak.

'I brought you here so that you could make public the latest development.'

63

'You brought me here?'

I can communicate to you on more than one conscious level, and some of your lower levels are very open to suggestion.

'I don't want to be here – I hate these people!'

So do I! You expect me to be born into this world among these zombies? What do you think I am? I'm not arriving till the world improves. I'll stay where I am for ever, do you hear?

That was the point at which Gordana had hysterics.

Eventually they got her out of the old church and into an ambulance. She was shot full of sedative and shipped down to her own living-level.

When she woke, she was in her own room, in her own bed, looking mountainous under the bedclothes. Randy was sitting by her, stroking her hand, and looking remarkably downcast. She thought perhaps he was reflecting on how long he had had to sleep on the floor because the bed was too full of her, but when he saw her eyes opening, he said bitterly, 'This jaunt of yours has cost us ninety-eight smackers on the public services. How are we going to pay that?'

Then, seeing he had hurt her, he tried to make up to her. He was sorry to be snide but he thought she had run away. He could not find a job, they might have to leave the flat, and weren't things just hell? In the end, they were both crying. Arms round each other, they fell asleep.

But without knowing it, Gordana had already solved their financial problems. The ambulance crew that shipped her home had reported her case to the Maternity Hospital, and now a thin stream of experts began to arrive at the flat – and not only gynaecologists, but a sociologist from Third Level University and a reporter from *Third Level News*. They all wanted to investigate Gordana's statement that her baby would not be born till the world improved. Since they lived in a cash society, Randy had no trouble at screwing money out of them before they could get in to see his wife. In a short while,

Gordana was news, and the interviews doubled. The cash flowed in and Randy bought himself a doorman's cap and smiled again.

'It's all very well for you, darling,' Gordana said one evening, as he strolled into the room and flung his hat into a corner. 'I get so tired telling them the same things over and over and posing for profile photos. When's it all going to end?'

'Cherub, I regret to say it's ending any moment now. We've had our day. You are news no longer! No longer are you a freak but one of many.'

She flung a cushion at him and stamped. 'I am not a freak and I never was a freak and you are just a miserable, horrible cheapskate little man to say I am!'

He leapt to her side and embraced as much of her as he could get his arms round.

'I didn't mean it, hon, really, not that way, you know I didn't, you know I love you, even if you are ten months gone. But look at the papers!'

He held a couple of coloureds out to her.

The story was all over the front page. Gordana was by no means the only pebble on the beach. No babies were being born all the way across the country, and there were hundreds of thousands of pregnancies of almost ten months' duration. Gordana's hysterics had triggered off the whole fantastic story. The medical world and the government were baffled or, as the headlines put it, STATE STALKS STORK STRIKE. One columnist was inclined to blame Comblok for the trouble, but that seemed hardly likely since a wave of unbirths was reported from all capitals of the world.

Gordana read every word carefully. Then she sprawled on the bed and looked her husband in the eye.

'Randy, there's no mention here of any woman being able to communicate with her unborn child the way I can.'

'Like I told you, honey, you're unique – that was the word I was looking for – unique.'

5   65

'I suspect all these mothers-to-be can talk with their babes same as I can. But you're the only person I told about that, and these women must feel as I do. It's a private thing. I want you to promise me you will not tell a soul I can talk to our baby. Promise?'

'Why, sure, hon, but what harm would it do? It wouldn't hurt you or junior.'

'It's woman's instinct, Randy, that's why, and that's reliable. People would only make capital out of it. Now, promise you'll keep the secret.'

'Sure, pet, I promise, but look, one of all these millions of expectant women is going to leak the secret, you know, and then it will not be a secret any more –'

'That's why it is essential to say nothing!'

' – But the guy – the gal who leaks it first could sure clean up a lot of dough if he leaked it to the right place!'

'Randy!'

'Why we could even move up into the upper levels, with daylight and all, the way you always wanted.'

'Randy, get out of my sight! Get out and don't come back! Haven't you made enough money already out of my misfortune without debasing us both? Get out and get yourself an honest job, and don't come back till you've got one.'

Randy sat drinking in a bar where they served a pretty strong shlivowitz, imported from Jugoslavia to save that country's economy, then in a state of crisis. The man with him was listening to what he said and buying him more shlivowitz; his name was Paddy van Dyck and he was Urban Psychology Romancer for the leading weekly *Mine*; he was saying, 'But let's get this clear, Mr Hicks, you say *you* never heard the baby speak?'

'Who's carrying it, her or me, I'd like to know? It's sort of telepathy, a telephone – I mean a telephone system, right up the bloodstream, just the two of them talking away, I'm left out of it completely, she doesn't want me any more, told me to clear out and get a job, doesn't love me any more.'

'Yes, so I believe you were saying earlier, Mr Hicks.'

Van Dyck brought a very large sum of money from his pocket. It had a sobering effect on Randy.

'This is for an immediate exclusive interview. No one else is to see your wife for purposes of interview for the next seven days. Understood?'

'Christ, yes. You have me convinced. Let me count it.'

'Let's go to your flat at once.'

But at the flats, Randy's courage failed. He recalled the promise he had made to Gordana so recently. In the hall, he caught sight of Sonia Greenslade, who nodded at him disapprovingly; she was putting on weight fast now. But van Dyck would allow no hesitation, and Randy was forced to open his door and march in.

A man was sitting on the bed beside Gordana.

'Hey! You're a fast worker, aren't you?' Randy exclaimed.

His wife gave him a dazzling smile and held out a puffy hand to him. 'Come along, darling! Where've you *been*? I thought things over and changed my mind about our little secret. This is Mr Maurice Tenberg of CB "Masterview", who is going to handle me exclusively for the next month.'

'For a considerable fee, Mr Hicks,' Tenberg said, rising and extending his hand. 'Your wife is a perspicacious business woman.'

By reflex, Randy held out his hand. It was stuffed with van Dyck's greenbacks. They were suddenly whipped away. Startled, he looked over his shoulder, in time to see van Dyck leave. The man knew when he was out-gunned.

The clutter of the cubision equipment in the hall was a considerable obstruction to the occupants of the flats, particularly those unfortunates like Sonia and John Greenslade on the same floor as the Hickses. As they climbed over cables or skirted trollies and monitor banks and powerpacks, they could see into the Hicks's room, which had lost the personality of its owners and was now a studio. Gordana's bed had given way to a fancy couch, and the cooking-equipment and sink were shrouded behind a wall-length curtain from the Props Department.

Gordana herself was heavily made up and dressed in a new gown. She was the star turn in an hour-long programme showing at a peak period on national networks. A panel of famous men had discussed the Baby Drought, as it was called, and now Maurice Tenberg was interviewing Gordana.

Subtly, he stressed both the human and the sensational side of the problem, the woman loving her child despite its irregularity, the novelty of a world into which no child had been born for six weeks, and now this remarkable new development where the mother could communicate subvocally with her infant. Finally, he turned to address the 3-D cameras direct.

'And now we are going to do something that has never been done before. We are going to attempt to interview a human being while it is still in the womb. I am going to ask Randy Junior questions, which will be relayed to him by Gordana. She will speak out loud to him, but I would like to emphasise that that is just for her convenience not his. Randy Junior shares her bloodstream and so appears able to have access to all the thought processes going on in her brain.'

Tenberg turned to Gordana and, addressing himself to her stomach, said, 'Can you tell us what sort of a world you are living in down there?'

Gordana repeated the question in a low voice. There was a long silence, and then she said, 'He says he lives in a great universe. He says he is like a thousand fish.'

'That's not a very clear answer. Ask him to answer more precisely. Is he aware of the difference between day and night?'

She put the question to him, and was aware of her child's answer growing like a tidal wave sweeping towards the shores of her understanding. Before it reached her, she knew it would overwhelm her.

The foetus within could vocalise thoughts no better than she could. But without words, it threw up at her a pictorial and sensory summary of its universe, a scalding hotchpotch of the environment in which it lived. Dark buildings from a thousand reveries, drowning faces, trees, household articles, landscapes that swelled grandly by like escaping oceans, an old ruined church, numberless, numberless people invaded her.

This was her son's world, gleaned from her, cast back – a world for him, floating in his cell without movement, which knew no dimensions of space. Everything, even the glimpses of widest desert or tallest building, came flattened in a strange two-dimensional effect, like the image dying in a cubision box when the tube blows. But if the embryo world had no space, it had its dimensions of time

In its reverie-life, the embryo had been free to drift in the deep reaches of its mother's mind, hanging beyond time where its mother's consciousness was unable to reach. It had no space, but it had, as it claimed, a great universe indeed!

As the flow of images smothered her, driving her into a deep faint, Gordana saw – knew – her mother, grandmother, great-grandmother – they were all there, seemingly at once, her female line, back and back, the most vividly remembered experience of a human life, faces looking down smiling, oddly similar, smiling, fading slowly as they flickered by, lowly faces at last, far back in lapsed time, their eyes still full of gentleness but at last no longer human, only small and shrewd and scared.

And over those maternal faces raced great gouts of light and shadow, as the cardinal facts of existence made themselves felt not as abstracts but as tangible things: birth and love and hunger and reproduction and warmth and cold and death. She was a mammal again, no longer a tiny unit in a grinding life-machine whose dark days were enacted before a background of plastic and brick: she was the live thing, a clever mammal, running from cold to warmth among the thronging animal kingdom, an animated pipeline from the distant past of sunlight and blood. She tried to cry at the magnificence and terror of what she felt . . . her mouth opened, only a faint animal sound emerged.

Of course, it made highly viewable CB. A doctor hurried on to the set and revived her, and in no time Tenberg was pressing ahead with the interview.

'He gave you a shock, didn't he, Gordana? What did your baby show you?'

With eyes closed, she said, 'The womb world. I saw the womb world. It is a universe. He is right . . . he has a freedom to live we have never known. Why should he want to be born from all that into this miserable cramped flat?'

'Your husband tells me you will be able to move up above ground soon,' Tenberg said, firmly cheerful. Gordana could not be said to respond to his tone.

'He can roam . . . everywhere. I'm just an ignorant woman and yet he can find in me a sort of wisdom that our brick and plastic civilisation has disqualified. . . . He's – oh, God! – he's more of a whole person than anyone I've ever met. He's seen – '

Observing that Gordana was on the brink of tears, Tenberg grasped her wrist and said firmly, 'Now, Gordana, we are wandering a little, and it is time we put another question to your son. Ask him when he is going to be born?'

Dutifully, she pulled herself together and repeated the question. She knew by his reply that Randy Junior too was exhausted by the attempt to communicate. His reply came back pale and without emotional tone, and she was able to repeat it aloud as he sub-vocalised.

'He says that he and all babies like him have decided not to be born into our world. It is our world, and we have made it and must keep it. They don't want it. It is too unpleasant a place for them. . . . I don't understand . . . oh, yes, he wishes us to pass on this message to all other

70

babies, that they are to control their feeding so that they grow no more and do not incapacitate their mothers further. From now on, they will remain as a parasitical subrace . . . '

Her voice faltered and died as she realised what was said. And it was this crucial statement on which everyone, almost throughout the world, dwelt next morning. This was the point, as an astute commentator was to remark, at which the Baby Drought developed from an amusing stunt to a national conspiracy – for Randy Junior has succeeded in communicating with all other unborn children through their watching mothers – and to a global disaster.

In the Hicks flat, panic broke out, and the producer of the show ran forward to silence Gordana. But she had something else to convey to the world from her son. Eyes shut, she raised one hand imperiously for silence and said, 'He says that to him and his kind, the foetuses, their life is the only life, the only complete life, the only life without isolation. The birth of a human being is the death of a foetus. In human religions which spoke of an afterlife, it was only a pale memory of the fore-life of the foetus. Hitherto, the human race has only survived by foeticide. Humans are dead foetuses walking. From now on, there will be only foetuses. . . . '

The crises, financial, political, national, ecumenical, educational, sociological, economic, and moral, through which the world was staggering, seemed as nothing after that. If the foetuses meant what they said, the human race was finished: there was a traitor literally within the gates.

In maternity hospitals, a series of emergency operations took place. Man could not bear to be defeated by mere unborn children. Everywhere, surgeons performed caesarean operations. Everywhere, the results were the same: the infants involved died. Frequently their mothers died with them. Within a few days, most countries had declared such operations illegal.

Gordana was immune from this wave of panic. She was too famous to be tampered with. She was made President of the Perpetually Pregnant, she was sent gifts and money and advice. Nevertheless, she remained downcast.

'Come on, hon, smile for Poppa!' Randy exclaimed, when he returned to the little flat a week after the momentous interview. Taking her in his arms, he said, 'Know what, Gordy, you and I are going topside to see your new flat! It's all fixed – well, it's not fixed, but we can take possession, and then we'll get it decorated and move in as soon as we can.'

'Darling Randy, you're so sweet to me!' she said sadly.

'Course I'm sweet to you, darling – who wouldn't be? But aren't you even going to ask me how many floors up we'll be? We're going to be fourteen floors above ground level! How do you like that? And we are going to have two rooms! How about that, hon?'

'It is wonderful, Randy.'

'Smile when you say that!'

They went to see the flat. The tenants had just died – at least the old lady had died and her husband had submitted to euthanasia – and everywhere was in a mess. But the view from the windows was fine and real sunlight came through them. All the same, Gordana remained low in spirits. It was as if life was a burden that was becoming too much for her to bear.

What with legal delays and decorators' delays, it was a month before Randy and Gordana Hicks moved into their new flat. On the last day in the old one, Gordana went and said a tearful goodbye to Sonia Greenslade, whose pregnancy was so well advanced that she and her child were communicating. She felt an unexpected reluctance to leave the old environment when the time came.

'You are happy here, Gordy?' Randy asked, when they had been installed for a week in their new home.

'Yes,' she said. She was sitting on a new couch that converted into a bed at night – no more cots that folded up into the ceiling. Randy sat on the window sill, looking

72

down at the teeming city. He did no work now and looked for none; money was in plentiful supply for once in their lives and he was making the most of the situation by doing nothing, and eating and drinking too much.

'You don't sound very happy, I'd say.'

'Well, I am. It's just – just that I feel we have sold ourselves, and the child.'

'We got a good price, didn't we?'

She winced at his cynicism. Slowly she got up, looking steadily at him. 'I'm going back down to the third level to see Sonia,' she said. 'We've got no friends on this level.'

'Tell me if I'm boring you!'

'Randy, I only said I was going to see Sonia.'

'Go on, then, don't make a song and dance about it – though you'd be hard put to dance in your state. For gosh sakes, Gordy, how goddamned long are you going to lumber about my life in that mountainous state?'

She faced him. 'Just so long as my baby wants it this way. The matter doesn't rest with you.'

He came down off the window sill. 'You know what I think? I think you are having an immoral affair with that foetus! I reckon I could divorce you on grounds – ' He stopped and grabbed her arms, hiding the pain on his face in her shoulder. 'I'm sorry, hon, I won't fly off the handle, I love you, you know, but how much longer are you damned women going to louse up the world?'

Sonia was delighted to see her old neighbour again. She invited Gordana in and they sat painfully at one end of the little room, close together, while John Greenslade sat at the other end of the room wrestling with the Bible and Western Civilisation. He was a small ragged man, not much taller than his wife and decidedly thinner. He sat in an old pair of slacks and a sweat-shirt, peering through his contact lenses at his phototape, occasionally uttering a sentence or two into it, but mainly scratching his head and muttering and playing back references in the mountains and alps of magnabooks piled round him. He paid no attention to the women.

'Mine's going to be a little boy – that is, I mean mine *is* a little boy, I mean to say. A little boy foetus,' Sonia confided, fluttering her eyelashes. 'I don't make him any garments and we haven't prepared a creche or anything – you do sort of save money that way, don't you think? His thoughts are coming on nicely, he talks quite well now – and he's not eight months yet, fancy! It is rather exciting, isn't it?'

'I don't know. I feel kind of depressed all the time.'

'My, that'll pass! Now you take me, I don't feel depressed at all, yet I'm much smaller than you, so I find Johnny heavy to carry. He seems to press down on my pelvis just *here*. Maybe when he's more responsive, I can get him to move round a bit. I get cramps, you know, can't sleep, get terribly restless, but no, I'm not a bit depressed. And you know what, Johnny already seems to take an interest in what John is writing. When John reads his stuff aloud, I can *feel* little Johnny drinks it all in. I don't think it's just my imagination, I can feel him drink it all in. He's going to be quite a little scholar!'

Gordana broke in on what threatened to become a monologue. 'Randy Junior doesn't talk much to me any more. I have a guilty feeling I lost his confidence when I let him be interviewed before all the world. But he's working away down there. Sometimes, I can't explain, but sometimes I feel he may be going to take me over and run me as if I were his automobile.'

'But we *are* their automobiles in a way, bless their sweet little hearts!'

'Sonia, I am not an automobile!'

'No, I didn't mean personally, naturally. But women – well, we women are used to being chattels, aren't we? Of men certainly, so why not of our babes?'

'You've been reading too much from the Bible!'

'As John always says, there was a lot of sense in that old book.'

'Will you confounded women keep your confounded voices down!' John shrieked, scattering reference books.

The days went by, and the weeks and months. No babies were born alive. The foetuses of the world had united. They preferred their vivid and safe pre-life to the hazards of human existence. The vast sums of money that the nations had hitherto devoted to defence were channelled increasingly into research on the birth problem.

Some of this money went to purchase the services of a noted psychiatrist, Mr Herbert Herbinvore, an immense pastoral man with shrewd eyes, a hairy mole on one cheek, and a manner so gentle it made him look like a somnambulist. He was appointed to get what sense he could out of Gordana, and they met for an hour every day.

In these sessions, Herbinvore coaxed Gordana into going over all her past life and into the reverie-life of her unborn child. He made copious notes, nodded wisely, closed his eyes, and went away smiling each morning at eleven-thirty.

When this had been going on for some weeks with no noticeable result, Gordana asked him, 'Are you coming to any conclusions yet, Herbert?'

He twinkled slightly at her. 'Surprisingly enough, yes. My assumptions are based on the opinion I have reached that you are a woman.'

'You don't say!'

'But I do say, my dear. It's something that mankind has never seriously taken into account – the femaleness of women, I mean. How did your foetus and every other foetus suddenly begin to communicate to you? Because that's what foetuses have always done with their mothers; that's why the months of pregnancy are such a dreamy time for most women. It has come to be a much more outward thing now because of the crisis, but women have always been in contact with the verities of life that little Randy exposed to you. Man is cut off from that, and has

75

to make the external world, without much aid from his womankind. It is, as they say, a man's world. More and more, these last centuries, the external world has ceased to resemble the reality that women know of subconsciously. When the conflict between the two opposites became sharp enough, the foetuses were jerked into a state of wakefulness by it – with the results we are now experiencing.'

Suddenly she was overcome with laughter. It seemed so silly, this fanciful stuff he was talking! As if he had any idea of what it was like to be a woman – yet he was telling her. 'And does – and does' – she controlled herself – 'does what you are saying now resemble most reality or the external world?'

'Mrs Hicks, you laugh like a sick woman! Man has adapted to his world, woman has failed to. Woman has stuck in the little reality-world. You take this matter too lightly. Unless you and all the other women like you pull yourselves together and deliver the goods, there isn't going to be any sort of reality to adjust to, because the human race will all be extinct.'

'How dare you call my son "goods"? He is an individual, and exists for his own self and not for any abstract like the human race. That's another man's notion if I ever heard one!'

He nodded so gently that it seemed he must rock himself to sleep. 'You more than confirm my diagnosis.'

They were both silent for a little while, and then Gordana asked, 'Herbert, have you ever read the Bible?'

'The Bible? It was long ago debunked as a work of cosmology, while as a handbook of etiquette it is entirely out of date. No, I haven't read it. Why do you ask?'

'A friend told me it says "Go forth and multiply". I wondered if maybe a woman wrote it?' And she started to laugh again. The sound of her son's voice within cut off her giggles.

'Mom, what is it like to be a man? Why is it so different?'

She had forgotten, as so often she did, that every conversation she had was available to Randy Junior as soon as it registered in her mind. 'Those are silly questions, darling. Go back to sleep,' she said.

'What did he ask?' Herbinvore enquired, looking more relaxed than ever.

'Never mind,' she muttered. Randy was repeating his questions. He repeated them after Herbinvore had left and throughout the afternoon, as though he could not believe there were things his omnipresent host did not know. He was only silenced when Sonia came to visit in the afternoon.

Sonia looked tearstained and dishevelled. She clutched at Gordana and looked at her wild-eyed.

'Is your husband here?'

'No. Out as usual.'

'Listen, Gordana, my poor little babykins has gone stark staring crazy! He wanted to know a whole lot of things I couldn't answer, and so I got John to answer, and then Johnny got interested in John's work, you know how they are. I just can't satisfy him. And now this morning — what do you think? — he ordered me to work at the phototaper when my husband was getting some sleep, and then he just took over my mind, and made me write the most utter nonsense!'

She waved a tape at Gordana. Gordana reached for it, but Sonia snatched it away.

'If you listen to it, you'll think my poor little baby has gone mad. He's digested everything from my husband's brain and scrambled it all up, and you'll think he's gone mad. As a matter of fact, I think he's gone mad. . . '

As she went into wails of misery, Gordana grabbed the tape and thrust it into the wall tapespeaker.

Sonia's voice filled the room — Sonia's voice, but barely recognisable as such, as it slowly pronounced its nonsense.

'Here no able, sow no able, spee no able, was the mogger of the three mogries, mescalin, feminine, and deuteronomy, and by their boots ye shall know them. And it

77

came to pass water, and darkness was over the face of the land, so that the land hid its face and could not look itself in the I, as was prophesied even in the days of the lesser prophets, particularly those born of the linen of Bluff King Hal, Hal King Bluff, and of course Bess Queen Good. Though she had the soul of a woman, she had the body of a man, kept in her privy where none should see. Woe to women who commit deuteronomy!

'The former treatise are shorter than the ones you are wearing, O excellent Thuck; yet, yea verily and between you and me and this magadeath, the royal lineage shall not pass away nor the land of the Ambisaurs which devour the sledded Politicians on the ice, nor the sun in the morning nor the moon in June, and as long as rivers cease to run this treaty shall stand between us though dynasties pass: you, you, and your airs and assigns and all who inherit, viz., your mother, your mother-in-law, daughter, female servant, ass, cow, sister, governess, god-daughter, or any other species of deuteronomous female, hereinafter referred to as The Publishers, shall not brew Liquor on the premises or allow anything to ferment or rot except on the third Sunday after Sexagesima, Boadecia, or Cleopatra, unto the third and fourth degeneration, for ever and ever, Amen.'

The silence grew in the room until Sonia said in her tiniest voice, 'You see, it's utterly meaningless. . . . '

'It seemed to me to have lots of – ' Gordana broke off. The foetus within her was making a noise like laughter; it said, *Now do you believe in Santa Claustrophobia!*

Urgently, Gordana said, 'I'm sorry, Sonia, you must get out of here, before you infect Randy Junior with the madness too. He is starting to talk nonsense as well.'

Without ceremony, she hustled her little bulging friend out of the door and leant against it, panting.

'You're going to try and scare us, aren't you?' she said aloud.

Do you suffer from negative geotropism? Remember

the fleas, climbing ever upward? You know what they were doing.'

'Annoying the swallows! But you're not going to be a flea, you're going to be a man.'

'The fleas were climbing upwards towards the light. Let there be light, let there be light!'

Whimpering softly, she crept over to the couch, lay down on it, and began meekly to give birth.

Randy Hicks, Herbert Herbinvore, Maurice Tenberg, the Mayor of the city, the Director of the Maternity Hospital, a gynaecologist and her assistant, three nurses, and an inquisitive shoeshine boy who happened to be passing stood round Gordana's bed, admiring her and her baby as they slept the deep sleep that only sedation can bring.

'She'll be just fine,' Herbinvore murmured to Randy, standing more relaxedly than most men sit. 'Everything is working out as I predicted. Don't forget, I was consulting your friend Sonia Greenslade every morning from eleven-thirty till twelve-thirty, and I could see how these foetuses were feeling. They liked their little world, but they were getting past it. Remember what your son was supposed to have said about a foetus having to die for a human to be born?'

Randy nodded mutely.

'Then picture how a human would feel if his life were unnaturally protracted to two hundred years; he would long for death and for what our superstitious ancestors would have called the Light Beyond. Young Randy felt like that. The time came when he had to overcome the forces ranged against him and move forth to be born.'

Randy pulled himself out of his daze. He longed to kneel and embrace his sleeping wife, but was cagey about the nurses who might laugh at him. 'Wait a bit, Doc, how do you mean he had to overcome the forces ranged against him? What forces? It was his idea not to get born in the first place.'

Only an old cow asleep in a meadow deep in grass

could have shaken her head as gently as Herbinvore did now in contradiction.

'No, no, no, I fear not. Things were not as they might have seemed to laymen like you. As I shall be saying to the world over the CB later tonight, the foetuses really had no option in the matter. The world was at crisis – half a dozen crises – and the women just suddenly came out with a mass neurosis. You might even say that world tension had paralysed women like Gordana, paralysed their uterine contractions so that labour could not take place. There are examples in the insect kingdom – among the flies, for instance – of creatures that can control their pregnancies until the moment is fit, so this incident is not entirely without precedent. It was the women that didn't want babies – nothing to do with what the babies felt at all.'

'But you heard what my kid – what Randy Junior said.'

'No, Mr Hicks, I did not. I never heard him utter a word. Nor did you. Nor did anyone else. We have only the word of the reluctant mothers that their babes spoke. That idea is all nonsense. Telepathy is nonsense, hogwash! The whole idea was just part and parcel of the womanly mass neurosis. Now that it looks as if the world's on the upgrade again, the girls are all giving birth. I'll guarantee that by tomorrow there's not a delayed pregnancy left!'

Randy felt himself compelled to scratch his head, but the whirling thoughts there refused to come to heel. 'Gosh!' he said.

'Precisely. I have it all diagnosed.' The grass in the meadow was well up to the cow's hocks. 'In fact, I will tell you something else – '

But Randy had already heard too much. Breaking away from the hypnotic sight of Herbinvore pontificating, he braved the nurses and flung himself down beside Gordana. Rousing gently, she wrapped an arm about him. The baby opened its blue eyes and looked at its father with a knowing and intelligent air.

Unperturbed, the psychiatrist continued to hold forth for the good of the company. 'I will tell you something else. When I had completed my diagnosis, I placed Mrs Greenslade under slight hypnosis to persuade her to write the nonsense she did. That was quite enough to scare the women into their senses again. . . . I have the feeling that possibly when this whole affair is written about in times to come, it may well be known as "Herbinvore's Syndrome". . . .'

The babe on the bed fixed him with a knowing eye.
'Nuts!' it said.

SEND HER VICTORIOUS

or

THE WAR AGAINST THE VICTORIANS, A.D. 2000

The news hit New York in time to feature in the afternoon editions. No editor splashed it very large, but there it was, clear enough on the front pages:

MANY DEATHS IN CASTLE CATASTROPHE
and
QUEEN'S HOME GONE
and
BRITAIN'S ENEMIES STRIKE?

Douglas Tredeager Utrect bought two papers as he fought his way to the Lexington Advanced Alienation Hospital, where he was currently engaged as Chief Advisor. The news did not tell him as much as he wished to know, which he found was generally the way with news. In particular, it did not mention his English friend, Bob Hoggart.

All that was said was that, during the early afternoon, a tremendous explosion which might be the work of hostile foreign powers had obliterated the grounds of the royal park of Windsor, Berkshire, England, and carried away most of Windsor Castle at the same time. Fortunately, the Queen was not in residence. Fifty-seven people were missing, believed killed, and the death roll was mounting. The Army was mobilising and the British Cabinet was meeting to discuss the situation.

Utrect had no time to worry over the matter, deeply though it concerned him. As soon as he entered his office in the Advanced Alienation Hospital, he was button-holed by Dr Froding.

'Ah, Utrect, there you are! Your severe dissociation case, Burton. He attacked the nurse! Quite inexplicable in such a quiet patient – rather, only explicable as anima-hostility, which hardly fits with his other behaviour. Will you come to see him?'

Utrect was always reluctant to see Burton. It alarmed him to discover how attracted he was by the patient's psychotic fantasy world. But Froding was not only a specialist on the anima; he was a forceful man. Nodding, Utrect followed him along the corridor, thrusting his moody reindeer's face forward as if scenting guilt and danger.

Burton sat huddled in one corner of his room – a characteristic pose. He was a pale slight man with a beard. This appeared to be one of his days when his attention was directed to the real world; his gestures towards it were courtly, and included the weariness which is so often a part of courtliness, although here it seemed more, Utrect thought, as if the man were beckoning distantly, and part of him issuing fading calls for help. Don't we all? he thought.

'We are pleased to receive your majesty,' Burton said, indicating the chair, secured to the floor, on which Utrect might sit. 'And how is the Empress today?'

'She is away at present,' Utrect said. He nodded towards Froding, who nodded back and disappeared.

'Ah, absent, is she? Absent at present. Travelling again, I suppose. A beautiful woman, the Empress, your majesty, but we must recognise that all her travelling is in the nature of a compulsion.'

'Surely, Herr Freud; but, if we may, I would much rather discuss your own case. In particular, I would like to know why you attacked your nurse.'

Burton looked conspiratorial. 'This Vienna of ours, your majesty, is full of revolutionaries these days. You must know that. Croats, Magyars, Bohemians – there is no end to them. This nurse girl was hoping to get at your majesty through me. She was in the pay of Serbian assassins.'

He was convinced that he was Sigmund Freud, although, with his small stature and little copper-coloured beard, he looked more like Algernon Charles Swinburne, the Victorian poet. He was convinced that Utrect was the Emperor Franz Josef of Austria. This confused mental state alternated with periods of almost complete catatonia. Year by year, the world's mental illnesses were growing more complex, spiralling towards ultimate uterine mindlessness, as the ever-expanding population radiated high dosages of psychic interference on all sides.

Although Burton's case was only one among many, its fascination-repulsion for Utrect was unique, and connected, directly but at a sub-rational level, with the commission on which he had sent Bob Hoggart to London, England. Many were the nights he had sat with Burton, humouring the man in his role, listening to his account of life in Vienna in the nineteenth century.

As a result, Utrect knew Vienna well. Without effort, he could hear the clatter of coaches in the streets, could visit the opera or the little coffee houses, could feel the cross-currents that drifted through the capital of the Hapsburgs from all corners of Europe. In particular, he could enter the houses, the homes. There was one home he loved, where he had seen a beautiful girl with a peacock feather; there, the walls were clear-coloured and plain, and the rooms light with dark-polished pieces of furniture. But he knew also the crowded homes of Freud's acquaintances, had made his way towards over-stuffed horse-hair sofas, knocking a Turkish rug from an occasional table, brushed past potted palms and ferns. He had sat and stared at dim volumes, too heavy to hold, which contained steel engravings of customs in the Bavarian Alps or scenes from the Khedive's Egypt. He had seen Johannes Brahms at a reception, listened to recitals of the Abbé Liszt and the waltzes of Johann Strauss. He knew – seemed to know – Elizabeth of Austria, Franz Josef's beautiful but unhappy wife, and occasionally found himself identifying her with his own doomed wife, Karen. He felt himself entirely at home in that distant Victorian world – far more at home than an alienist with an international reputation in the year 2000 should be.

This afternoon, as Burton rambled on about treason and conspiracies at court, Franz Josef's attention wandered. He had an illusion much greater than one man's madness to diagnose. He knew that he, his companions, his ailing wife, the great bustling world, faced imminent disaster. But he continued to dispense automatic reassurance, while sustaining the role of the Emperor.

As he left Burton at last, Froding happened to be passing along the corridor. 'Does he seem disturbed?'

'I cannot make sense of the fellow,' Utrect said. Then he recalled himself. He was not the Emperor, and must not talk like him. 'Er – he is quiet at present, probably moving towards withdrawal. Pulse rate normal. See that he is monitored on "A" Alert tonight.'

Dismissing Froding rather curtly, he hurried to his office. He could catch a news bulletin in four minutes. He flicked on the desk 3V and opened up his wrisputer, feeding it the nugatory data contained in the paper report on Windsor Castle. He added to the little computer, 'More details when the newscast comes up. Meanwhile, Burton. He attacked his nurse, Phyllis. In his Freud persona, he claims that she was a revolutionary. Revolution seems to be dominating his thinking these days. He also claims an anti-semitic conspiracy against him at the university. Multi-psychotic complex of persecution-theme. Indications his mental condition is deteriorating.'

Switching off for a moment, Utrect swallowed a pacifier. Everyone's mental condition was deteriorating as the environment deteriorated. Burton had simply been cheated out of the presidency of a little tin-pot society he had founded; that had been enough to topple him over the brink. Utrect dismissed the man from his mind.

He ignored the adverts scampering across the 3V screen and glanced over the routine daily bulletins of the hospital piled on his desk. Under the new Dimpsey Brain Pressure ratings, the figures in all wards were up at least .05 over the previous day. They had been increasing steadily, unnervingly, for a couple of years, but this was the biggest jump yet. The World Normality Norm had been exceeded once more; it would have to be bumped up officially again before alarm spread. By the standards of the early nineties, the whole world was crazy; by the standards of the seventies, it was one big madhouse. There were guys now running banking houses, armies, even major industries, who were proven round the bend in one or more (generally many more) of three thousand two hundred and six Dimpsey ways. Society was doing its best to come to terms with its own madness; more than one type of paranoia was held to be an inescapable qualification for promoting in many business organisations.

The oily voice seeping from the 3V screen asked, 'Ever feel this busy world is too much for you? Ever want to scream in the middle of a crowd? Ever want to murder everyone else in your apartment building? Just jab a Draculin. . . . Suddenly, you're all alone! . . . Just jab a Draculin. . . . Remember, when you're feeling over-populated, just jab a Draculin. . . . Suddenly, you're all alone!' Drug-induced catatonia was worth its weight in gold these days.

Struggling under all his responsibilities, acknowledged or secret, Utrect could admit to the fascination of that oily syren voice. He was burdened with too many roles. Part of his morbid attraction to the Burton case lay in the fact that he liked being Franz Josef, married to the beautiful Elizabeth. It was the most restful part of his existence!

The oily voice died, the news flared. Utrect switched on his wrisputer to record. A picture of Windsor Castle as it had been tumesced from the 3V and confronted Utrect. He stared tensely, omitting to blink, as shots of the disaster came up. There was very little left of the residence of the anachronistic British sovereigns, except for one round tower. The demolition was amazing and complete. No rubble was left, no dust: just level ground where the building and part of the town had been.

The commentator said, 'The historic castle was only on the fringe of a wide area of destruction. Never before has one blow destroyed so much of the precious British heritage. Historic Eton College, for centuries the breeding-ground of future aristocrats, has been decimated. Shrine of world-famous historic nineteenth-century Queen Victoria, at Frogmore, situated one mile south-east of the castle, was wiped out completely.

Bob Hoggart! I sent you to your death! Utrect told himself. He switched off, unwilling to listen to the fruitless discussion about which enemy nation might have knocked off the castle; *he* knew what had wrought the terrible destruction.

'Hoggart,' he said to the wrisputer. 'You had a record of his probable movements at the time when disaster struck Windsor. What are your findings?'

The little machine said, 'Hoggart was scheduled to spend day working at Royal Mausoleum and – to cover his main activity – investigating nearby cemetery adjoining mausoleum, in which lesser royalties are buried. At time destruction happened, Hoggart may have been actually at Royal Mausoleum. Prediction of probability of death, based on partial data: fifty-six point oh nine per cent.'

Burying his face in his hands, Utrect said, 'Bob's dead then. . . . My fault. . . . My guilt, my eternal damned guilt. . . . A murderer – worse than a murderer! Hoggart was just a simple but courageous little shrine-restorer, no more. Yet subconsciously I manoeuvred him into a position where he was certain to meet his death. Why? Why? Why do I actually hate a man I thought I really liked? Some unconscious homosexual tendencies maybe, which had to be killed?' He sat up. 'Pull yourself together,

88

Douglas! You are slumping into algolagnic depression, accentuated by that recurrent guilt syndrome of yours. Hoggart was a brave man, yes; you ordered him to go to Windsor, yes; but you in turn had your orders from the PINCS. There is no blame. These are desperate times. Hoggart died for the world — as the rest of us will probably do. Besides, he may not be dead after all. I must inform PINCS. Immediately.'

One thing at least was clear, one thing at least stood out in fearful and uncompromising hues: the universe lay nearer to the brink of disaster than ever before. The dreaded Queen Victoria had struck, and might be about to strike again.

The United States, in the year 2000, was riddled with small and semi-secret societies. All of its four hundred million inhabitants belonged to at least one such society; big societies, like the Anti-Procreation League; small ones, like the Sons of Alfred Bester Incarnate; crazy ones, like the Ypslanti Horse-Hooves-and-All-Eating Enclave; dedicated ones, like the Get Staff; religious ones, like the Man's Dignity and Mulattodom Shouting Church; sinister ones, like the Impossible Smile; semi-scholarly ones, like the Freud In His Madness Believers, which the insane Burton had founded; save-the-world ones, like All's Done In Oh One Brotherhood.

It was in the last category that the Philadelphia Institute for Nineteenth Century Studies belonged. Behind the calm and donnish front of PINCS, a secret committee worked, a committee comprising only a dozen men drawn from the highest and most influential ranks of cosmopolitan society. Douglas Tredeager Utrect was the humblest member of this committee: the humblest, and yet his aim was theirs, his desire burned as fiercely as theirs: to unmask and if possible annihilate the real Queen Victoria.

Committee members had their own means of communication. Utrect left the Advanced Alienation Hospital and headed for the nearest call-booth, plunging through the crowded streets, blindly pushing forward. He was wearing his elbow guards but, even so, the sidewalk was almost unendurable. The numbers of unemployed in New York City were so great, and the space in their over-crowded flats and rooms so pronounced, that half the family at any one time found life more tolerable just padding round the streets.

To Utrect's disgust, a married couple, the woman with an eighteen-month-old child still being breast-fed, had moved into the call-booth; they were employees of the Phone Company and had evidence of legal residence. However, since Utrect could show that this was an hour when he could legitimately make a call, they had to turn out while he dialled.

He got three wrong numbers before Disraeli spoke on the other end. The visiscreen remained blank; it was in any case obscured by a urine-soaked child's nightshirt. Disraeli was a PINCS' code name; Utrect did not know the man's real one. Sometimes, he suspected it was none other than the President of the United States himself.

'Florence Nightingale here,' Utrect said, identifying himself, and said no more. He had already primed his wrisputer. It uttered a scream lasting point six of a second.

A moment's silence. A scream came back from Disraeli's end. Utrect hung up and scarpered, leaving the family to take possession again.

To get himself home fast, he called a rickshaw. Automobiles had been banned from the city centre for a decade now; rickshaws provided more work for more people. Of course, you had to be Caucasian Protestant to qualify for one of the coveted rickshaw-puller's licenses.

He was lucky to qualify for a luxury flat. He and his wife, Karen, had three rooms on the twenty-fifth floor of the Hiram Bucklefeather Building – high enough to evade some of the stink and noise of the streets. The elevator generally functioned too. Only the central-heating had failed; and that would have been no bother in mild fall weather had not Karen been cyanosis-prone.

She was sitting reading, huddled in an old fur coat, as Utrect entered the flat.

'Darling, I love you!' she said dimly, glancing up, but marking her place on the page with a blueish fingertip. 'I've missed you so.'

'And me you.' He went to wash his hands at the basin, but the water was off.

'Have a busy day, darling?' At least she pretended to be interested.

'Sure.' She was already deep back in – he saw the title because she, as undeviatingly intellectual now as the day he married her, held it so that he might see – *Symbolic Vectors in Neurasthenic Emotional Stimuli*. He made a gesture towards kissing the limp hair on her skull.

'Good book?'

'Mm. Absorbing.' Invalidism had sapped her ability to tell genuine from false. Maybe the only real thing about us is our pretences, Utrect thought. He patted Karen's shoulders; she smiled without looking up.

Cathie was in the service-room-cum-bedroom, sluggishly preparing an anaemic-looking piece of meat for their supper. She was no more substantial than Karen, but there was a toughness, a masculine core, about her, emphasized by her dark skin and slight, downy moustache. Occasionally, she showed a sense of humour. Utrect patted her backside; it was routine.

She smiled. 'Meat stinks of stilbestrol these days.'

'I didn't think stilbestrol had any odour.'

'Maybe it's the stilbestrol stinks of meat.'

They'd done okay, he thought as he locked himself in the bathroom-toilet. They'd done okay. With his two sons, Caspar and Nero, they were a household of five, minimum number in relation to floor-space enforced by the housing regulations. Karen and Cathie had enjoyed a lesbian relationship since graduate days, so it was natural to have Cathie move in with them. Give her her due, she integrated well. She was an asset. Nor was she averse to letting Utrect explore her hard little body now and then.

He dismissed such sympathetic thoughts and turned his attention to the wrisputer, which slowed Disraeli's phoned scream and retransmitted it as a comprehensible message:

'Whether or not Robert Hoggart managed to fulfil his mission at the Windsor Mausoleum is immaterial. Its sudden destruction is conclusive proof that he, and we, were on the right track with our Victorian hypothesis. We now operate under Highest Emergency conditions. Secret PINCS messengers are already informing Pentagon in Washington and our allies in the Kremlin in Moscow. Now that the entity known as Queen Victoria has revealed her hand like this, she will not hesitate to distort the natural order again. The fact that she has not struck until this minutes seems to indicate that she is not omniscient, so we stand a chance. But clearly PINCS is doomed if she has discovered our secret. You will stand by for action, pending word from Washington and Moscow. Stay at home and await orders. Out.'

As he switched off, Utrect was trembling. He switched on again, getting the wrisputer to launch into a further episode of the interminable pornographic story it had been spinning Utrect for years; it was a great balance-restorer; but at the moment there was a banging at the toilet door, and he was forced to retreat.

He was a man alone. The Draculin situation, he thought wryly. Alone, and hunted. He looked up at the seamed ceiling apprehensively. That terrible entity they called Queen Victoria could strike through there, at any time.

The sons came home from work, Caspar first, thin, strawy, colourless save for the acne rotting his cheeks. Even his teeth looked grey. He was silent and nervous. Nero came in, two years the younger, as pallid as his brother, blackheads and adolescent pimples rising like old burial mounds from the landscape of his face. He was as talkative as Casper was silent. Grimly, Utrect ignored them. He had some thinking to do. Eventually, he retreated into the shower, sitting on the cold tiles. Queen Victoria might not see him there.

The evening dragged by. He was waiting for something and did not know what, although he fancied it was the end of the world.

The doomed life of the place slithered past. Utrect wondered why most of the tenants of the Hiram Buckle-feather Building had harsh voices. He could hear them through the walls, calling, swearing, suffering. Cathie and Karen were playing cards. At least the Utrect apartment preserved reasonable quiet.

Utrect's sons, heads together, indulged in their new hobby. They had joined the Shakespeare-Spelling Society. Their subscription entitled them to a kit. They had built the kit into an elaborate rat-educator. Two rats lived in the educator; they had been caught in the corridor. The rats had electrodes implanted in the pleasure centres of their brains. They were desperate for this pleasure and switched on the current themselves; when it was on, the happy creatures fed themselves up to seven shocks a second, their pink paws working the switches in a frenzy of delight.

But the current was available only when the rats spelt the name SHAKESPEARE correctly. For each of the eleven letters the rats had a choice of six letters on a faceted drum. The letters they chose were flashed on to a little screen outside the educator. The rats knew what they were doing, but, in their haste to get the coveted shock, they generally misspelled, particularly towards the end of the word. Casper and Nero tittered together as the mistakes flashed up.

THAMEZPEGE

SHAKESPUNKY

SRAKISDOARI

The Utrect tribe ate their stilbestrol steak. Since the water supply was on, Karen washed up, wearing her coat still. Utrect had thought he might take a walk when the pedestrians thinned a little, despite PINGS' orders, but it

93

was too late now. The hoods were out there, making the night unsafe even for each other. Every eight days, New York City needed one new hospital, just to cope with night-injuries, said the statistics.

MHAKERPEGRE

SHAKESPEAVL

Utrect could have screamed. The rats played on his latent claustrophobia. Yet he was diverted despite himself, abandoning thought, watching the crazy words stumble across the screen. He thought as he had often thought: supposing man did not run the goddamned rats? Supposing the goddamned rats ran men? There were reckoned to be between three and four million people already in the Shakespeare-Spelling Society. Supposing the rats were secretly working away down there to make men mad, beaming these crazy messages which men were forced to read and try to make some sort of meaning of? When everyone was mad, the rats would take over. They were taking over already, enjoying their own population explosion, disease-transmitting but disease resistant. As it was, the rats had fewer illusions than the boys. Caspar and Nero had a rat-educator; therefore they believed they were educating rats.

SIMKYSPMNVE

SHAKESPEARE

The Bard's name stayed up in lights when the rodents hit the currentjackpot and went on a pleasure binge, squealing with pleasure, rolling on their backs, showing little white thighs as the current struck home. Utrect refused to deflect his thoughts as Cathie and the boys crowded round to watch. Even if these rats were under man's surveillance, they were not interfered with by man once the experiment was set up. The food that appeared in their hoppers must seem to do so by natural law to them, just as the food thrusting out of the ground came by a natural law to mankind. Supposing man's relationship to Queen Victoria was analogous to the rats' relationship to man? Could they possibly devise some system to drive HER crazy, until she lost control of her experiment?

Pleasure was brief, sorrow long, in this vale of rodential tears. Now the creatures had to pick up the pieces and begin again. They had always forgotten after the pleasure-bout.

DRALBUCEEVE

The family all slept in the same room since Utrect had caught the boys indulging in forbidden activity together. Their two hammocks now swung high over the bed in which the women slept. Utrect had his folding bunk by the door, against the cooker. Often, he did not sleep well, and could escape into the living-room. Tonight, he knew, he would not sleep.

He dreamed he was in the Advanced Alienation Hospital. He was going to see Burton, pushing through the potted palms to get to the patient. An elderly man was sitting with Burton; Burton introduced him as his superior, Professor Krafft-Ebbing of Vienna University.

'Delighted,' Utrect murmured.

'Clukyzpegpy,' said the professor. 'And dralbuceeve.' What a thing to say to an Emperor!

Groaning, Utrect awoke. These crazy dreams! Maybe he was going mad; he knew his Dimpseys were already pushing the normality norm. Suddenly it occurred to him that the whole idea of Queen Victoria's being a hostile entity in a different dimension was possibly an extended delusion, in which the other members of PINCS conspired. A mother-fear orgy. A multiple mother-fear orgy – induced by the maternal guilt-aspects of over-population. He lay there, trying to sort fantasy from reality, although convinced that no man had ever managed the task to date. Well, Jesus, maybe; but if the Queen Victoria hypothesis was correct, then Jesus never existed. All was uncertain. One thing was clear, the inevitable chain of events. If the hypothesis was correct, then it could never have been guessed earlier in the century, when normality norms were lower. Over-population had brought universal

95

neurosis; only under such conditions could men reasonably work on so untenable a theory.

The Cheyne-Stokes breathing of his wife came to him, now labouring heavily and noisily, now dying away altogether. Poor dear woman, he thought; she had never been entirely well; even now, she was not entirely ill. In somewhat the same way, he had never loved her wholeheartedly; but even now, he had not ceased to love her entirely.

Tired though he was, her frightening variations of breathing would not let him rest. He got up, wrapped a blanket round him, and padded into the next room. The rats were still at work. He looked down at them.

SLALEUPEAKE

SLAKEBUDDVS

Sometimes, he tried to fathom how their sick little brains were working. The Shakespeare-Spelling Society issued a monthly journal, full of columns of misspelling of the Bard's name sent in by readers; Utrect pored over them, looking for secret messages directed at him. Sometimes the rodents in their educator seemed to work relaxedly, as if they knew the desired word was bound to come up after a certain time. On other occasions, they threw up a bit of wild nonsense, as if they were not trying, or were trying to cure themselves of the pleasure habit.

DOAKERUGAPE

FISMERAMNIS

Yes, like that, you little wretches, he thought.

The success of the Shakespeare-Spelling Society had led to imitations, the All-American-Spelling, the Rat-Thesaurus-Race, the Anal-Oriented-Spelling, and even the Disestablishmentarianism-Spelling Society. Rats were at work everywhere, ineffectually trying to communicate with man. The de-luxe kits had chimps instead of rats.

SHAPESCUNRI

SISEYSPEGRE

Tiredly, Utrect wondered if Disraeli might signal to him through the tiny screen.

The exotic words flickered above his head. He slept, skull resting on folded arms, folded arms resting on table.

Burton was back as Freud, no longer disconsolate as the sacked president of the Freud In His Madness Believers but arrogant as the arch-diagnoser of private weaknesses. Utrect sat with him, smoking in a smoking-jacket on a scarlet plush sofa. It was uncertain whether or not he was Franz Josef. There were velvet curtains everywhere, and the closed sweet atmosphere of a high-class brothel. A trio played sugary music; a woman with an immense bust came and sang a poem of Grillparzer's. It was Vienna again, in the fictitious nineteenth century.

Burton/Freud said, 'You are sick, Doctor Utrect, or else why should you visit this church?'

'It's not a church.' He got up to prove his point, and commenced to peer behind the thick curtains. Behind each one, naked couples were copulating, though the act seemed curiously indistinct and not as Utrect visualised it. Each act diminished him; he grew smaller and smaller. 'You're shrinking because you think they are your parents,' Burton/Freud said superciliously.

'Nonsense,' Utrect said loudly, now only a foot high. 'That could only be so if your famous theory of psycho-analysis were true.'

'If it isn't true, then why are you secretly in love with Elizabeth of Austria?'

'She's dead, stabbed in Geneva by a mad assassin. You'll be saying next I wish I'd stabbed my mother, or similar nonsense.'

'You said it – I didn't! Stabbed is good!'

'Your theories only confuse matters.'

An argument developed. He was no higher than Freud's toecap now. He wanted to pop behind a pillar and check to see if he was not also changing sex.

'There is no such thing as the subconscious,' he declared. Freud was regarding him now through pink reflecting glasses, just like the ones Utrect's father had worn.

Indeed, it came as no surprise to see that Freud, now sitting astride a gigantic smiling sow, *was* his father. Far from being nonplussed, the manikin pressed his argument even more vigorously.

'We have no subconscious. The Nineteenth Century is our subconscious, and you stand as our guardian to it. The Nineteenth Century ended in 1901 with the death of Queen Victoria. And of course it did not really exist, or all the past ages in which we have been made to believe. They are memories grafted on, supported by fake evidence. The world was invented by the Queen in 1901 – as she had us call that moment of time.'

Since he had managed to tell the truth in his dream, he began to grow again. But the hairy creature before him said, 'If the Nineteenth Century is your subconscious, what acts as the subconscious of the Victorians?'

Utrect looked about among the potted palms, and whispered. 'As *we* had to invent mental science, *you* had to invent the prehistoric past – that's your subconscious, with its great bumping monsters!'

And Burton was nodding and saying, 'He's quite right, you know. It's all a rather clumsy pack of lies.'

But Utrect had seen that the potted palms were in fact growing out of the thick carpets, and that behind the curtains stalked great unmentionable things. The velvet drapes bulged ominously. A great stegosaurus, lumbering, and rounder than he could have imagined, plodded out from behind the sofa. He ran for his life, hearing its breathing rasp behind him. Everything faded, leaving only the breathing, that painful symptom of anaemia, the Cheyne-Stokes exhalations of his wife in the next room. Utrect sprawled in his chair, tranquil after the truth-bringing nightmare, thinking that they (Queen Victoria) had not worked skilfully enough. The mental theories of 2000 were organised around making sense of the mad straggle of contradiction in the human brain. In fact, only the Queen Victoria hypothesis accounted for the contradictions. They were the scars left when the entirely artificial set-up of the world was commenced at the moment they perforce called 1901. Mankind was not what it seemed; it was a brood of rats with faked memories, working in some gigantic educator experiment.

SHAKESPEGRL

SHAKERPEAVE

Like the rats, he felt himself near to the correct solution. Yes! Yes, by God! He stood up, almost guilty, smiling, clutching the blanket to his chest. Obviously, analytic theory, following the clues in the scarred mind, could lead to the correct solution, once one had detected the 1901 barrier. And he saw! He knew! They were all cavemen, stone-age men, primitive creatures, trying to learn – *what?* – for the terrible woman in charge of this particular experiment. Didn't all mental theory stress the primitive side of the mind? Well, they were primitive! As primitive and out of place as a stegosaurus in a smoking-room.

SHAKESPEARL

Shakespearls before swine, he thought. He must cast his findings before PINCS before *She* erased him from the experiment. Now that he *knew*, the Queen would try to kill him as she had Hoggart.

There it was again. . . . He went to the outer door. He had detected a slight sound. Someone was outside the flat, listening, waiting. Utrect's mind pictured many horrible things. The stegosaurus was lying in wait, maybe.

'Douglas?' Dinosaurs didn't talk.

'Who is it?' They were whispering through the hinge.

'Me. Bob, Bob Hoggart!'

Shaking, Utrect opened up. Momentary glimpse of dim-lit corridor with homeless people snoozing in corners, then Hoggart was in. He looked tired and dirty. He staggered over to the table and sat down, his shoulders slumping. The polished restorations expert looked like a fugitive from justice.

SHAMIND

Utrect cut off the rats' source of light.

99

'You shouldn't have come here!' he said. 'She'll destroy this building – maybe the whole of New York!'

Hoggart read the hostility and fear in Utrect's expression.

'I had to come, Florence Nightingale! I jumped a jumbo-jet from London. I had to bring the news home personally.'

'We thought you were dead. PINCS thinks you're dead.'

'I very nearly am dead. What I saw . . . Give me a drink, for God's sake! What's that noise?'

'Quiet! It's my wife breathing. Don't rouse her. She suffers from haemoglobin-deficiency with some other factors that haven't yet been diagnosed. One of these new diseases they can't pin down –'

'I didn't ask for a case history. Where's that drink?' Hoggart had lost his English calm. He looked every inch a man that death had marked.

'What have you found?'

'Never mind that now! Give me a drink.'

As he drank the alcohol-and-water that Utrect brought him, Hoggart said, 'You heard she blasted the mausoleum and half Windsor out of existence? That was a panic move on her part – proves she's human, in her emotions at least. She was after me, of course.'

'The tomb, man – what did you find?'

'By luck, one of the guards happened to recognise me from an occasion when I was restoring another bit of architecture where he had worked before. So he left me in peace, on my own. I managed to open Queen Victoria's tomb, as we planned.'

'Yes! And?'

'As we thought!'

'Empty?'

'Empty! Nothing. So we have our proof that the Queen as history knows her – our fake history – does not exist.'

'Another of her botches, eh? Like the Piltdown Man and the Doppler Shift and the tangle of nonsense we call Relativity. Obvious frauds! So she's clever, but not all

100

that clever. Look, Bob, I want to get you out of here. I'm afraid this place will be struck out like Windsor at any minute. I must think of my wife.'

'Okay. You know where we must go, don't you?' He stood up, straightened his shoulders.

'I shall phone Disraeli and await instructions. One thing – how come you escaped the Windsor blast?'

'That I can't really understand. Different time scales possibly, between her world and ours? Directly I saw the evidence of the tomb, I ran for it, got into my car, drove like hell. The blast struck almost exactly an hour after I opened the tomb I was well clear of the area by then. Funny she was so unpunctual. I've been expecting another blast ever since.'

Utrect was prey to terrible anxiety. His fingers trem bled convulsively as he switched off his wrisputer, in which this conversation was now recorded. Before this building was destroyed, with Karen and all the innocent people in it, he had to get Hoggart and himself away. Grabbing his clothes, he dressed silently, nodding a silent good-bye to his wife. She slept with her mouth open, respiration now very faint. Soon, he was propelling Hoggart into the stinking corridor and down into the night. It was two-thirty in the morning, the time when human resistance was lowest. He instinctively searched the sky for a monstrous regal figure.

Strange night cries and calls sounded in the canyons of the streets. Every shadow seemed to contain movement. Poverty and the moral illness of poverty settled over everything, could almost be felt; the city was an analogue of a sick subconscious. Whatever her big experiment was, Utrect thought, it sure as hell failed. The cavemen were trying to make this noble city as much like home territory as they could. Their sickness (could be it was just home-sickness?) hung in the soiled air.

By walking shoulder-to-shoulder, flick-knives at the alert, Utrect and Hoggart reached the nearby call-booth without incident.

'Night emergency!' Utrect said, flinging open the door. The little family were sleeping in papoose hammocks, hooked up behind their shoulderblades, arms to their sides, like three great chrysalids. They turned out, sleepy and protesting. The child began to howl as its parents dragged it on to the chilly sidewalk.

Hoggart prepared a wrisputer report as Utrect dialled Disraeli. When his superior's throaty voice came up – again no vision – Hoggart let him have the scream. After a pause for encoding, another scream came from the other end. The wrisputer decoded it. They had to state present situation. When they had done this, a further scream came back. The matter was highest priority. They would be picked up outside the booth in a couple of minutes.

'Can we come back in, mister? The kid's sick!'

Utrect knew how the man felt.

As they bundled in, Utrect asked, 'When are you getting a real place?'

'Any year now, they say. But the company's agreed to heat the booth this winter, so it won't be so bad.'

We all have blessings to count, Utrect thought. Until the experiment is called off ...

He and Hoggart stood outside, back to back. A dark shape loomed overhead. A package was lowered. It contained two face masks. Quickly, they put them on. Gas flooded down, blanketing the street. A whirler lowered itself and they hurried aboard, immune from attacks by hoods, to whom a whirler would be a valuable prize. They lifted without delay.

Dr Randolph Froding's lips were a thin pale scarlet. As he laughed, little bubbles formed on them, and a thin spray settled on the glass of the television screen.

'This next part of my experiment will be very interesting, you'll see, Controller,' he said, glancing up, twinkling, at Prestige Normandi, Controller of the Advanced Alienation Hospital, a bald, plump man currently trying to look rather gaunt. Normandi did not like Dr Froding, who constantly schemed for the controllership. He watched with a jaundiced eye as, on Froding's spy screen, the whirler carried Hoggart and Chief Adviser Utrect over the seamy artery of the Hudson.

'I can hardly watch any longer, Froding,' he said, peering at his wrisputer. 'I have other appointments. Besides, I do not see you have proved your point.'

Froding tugged his sleeve in an irritating way.

'Just wait and watch this next part, Controller. This is where you'll see how Dimpsey Utrect really is.' He mopped the screen with a Kleenex, gesturing lordly with it as if to say, 'Be my guest, look your fill!'

Normandi fidgeted and looked; Froding was a forceful man.

They both stared as, in the 3V, the whirler could be seen to land on a bleak wharf, where guards met Utrect and Hoggart and escorted them into a warehouse. The screen blanked for a moment and then Froding's spy flipped on again, showing Utrect and Hoggart climbing out of an elevator and into a heavily guarded room, where a bulky man sat at a desk.

'I'm Disraeli,' the bulky man said.

Froding nudged the Controller. 'This is the interesting part, Controller! See this new character? Notice anything funny about him? Watch this next bit and you'll see what I'm getting at.'

On the screen, Disraeli was shaking hands with Hoggart and Utrect. He wore the uniform and insignia of a general. He led the two newcomers into an adjoining room, where ten men stood stiffly round a table.

Bowing, Disraeli said, 'These are the other members of our secret committee. May I introduce Dickens, Thackeray, Gordon, Palmerston, Gladstone, Livingstone, Landseer, Ruskin, Raglan, and Prince Albert, from whom we all take our orders.'

As Utrect and Hoggart moved solidly round the group, shaking hands and making the secret sign, distant Machiavellian Dr Froding chuckled and sprayed the screen again.

'At last I'm proving to you, Controller, what I've been saying around the Lexington for years – Utrect is clean Dimpsey.'

'He looks normal enough to me.' Dirty little Froding; so clearly after Utrect's job as well as Normandi's own.

'But observe the others, Prince Albert, Disraeli, and the rest! They aren't real people, you know, Controller. You didn't think they were real people, did you? Utrect thinks they are real people, but in fact they are dummies, mechanical dummies, and Utrect is talking to them as if they were real people. That proves his insanity, I think?'

Taken aback, Normandi said, ' . . . Uh . . . I really have to go now, Froding.' Horrified by this glimpse into Froding's mentality, Normandi excused himself and almost ran from the room.

Froding shook his head as the Controller hurried away. 'He too, poor schmuck, he too is near his upper limit. He will not last long. It's all this overcrowding, of course, general deterioration of the environment. The mentality also deteriorates.'

He had his own method of safeguarding his own sanity. That was why he had become a member of the Knights of the Magnificent Microcosm. Although, as a bachelor, he was allowed only this one small room with shared conveniences with the specialist next door, he had rigged up internal 3V circuits in it so as to enlarge his vistas enormously. Leaning back, Froding could look at a bank of three unblinking screens, each showing various parts of the room in which he sat. One showed a high view of the room from above the autogrill, looking down on Froding from the front and depicting also the worn carpet and part of the rear wall where there hung a grey picture executed by a victim of animahostility. One showed a view across the length of the room from behind the door, with the carpet, part of the table, part of the folding-bed, and the corner in which Froding's small personal library, together with his voluminous intimate personal dream diary, was housed in stacked tangerine crates. One showed a view from a corner, with the carpet, the more comfortable armchair, and the back of Froding's head as he sat in the chair, plus the three screens on which he was watching the three views of his room which included a view of him watching the three screens in his room on which he was watching this magnificent microcosm.

Meanwhile, at the subterranean PINCS HQ, Utrect had recognised Prince Albert; it was the Governor of New York city.

'We have a brief report of your activities in England, Hoggart,' Albert said. 'One question. How come you took so long to get here? You know how vital it was to alert us.'

Hoggart nodded. 'I got away from Victoria's mausoleum before the destruction, as I told Nightingale and Disraeli. The information I thought I ought to reserve until I could talk to a top authority like yourself, sir, was this. Once Windsor and the Royal Mausoleum were destroyed, I believed I might be safe for an hour or two. So I went back.'

'You went back to the devastated area?'

The Englishman inclined his head. 'I went back to the devastated area. You see, I was curious to find out whether the Queen – as I suppose we must continue to call her – had been trying to obliterate me or the evidence. It was easy to get through the police and military cordon; it was only just going up, and the devastation covers several square miles. Finally, I got to the spot where I judged the mausoleum had stood. Sure enough, the hole under the vault was still there.'

'What is so odd about this hole?' Dickens asked, leaning forward.

'It's no ordinary hole. I didn't really have time to look into it properly, but it – well, it baffles the sight. It's as if one were looking into a space – well, a space with more

105

dimensions than ours; and that's just what I suspect it is. It's the way – a way, into Queen Victoria's world.'

There was a general nodding of heads. Palmerston said in a crisp English voice, 'We'll take your word for it. Each of us bears a navel to indicate our insignificant origins. This hole you speak of may be Earth's navel. It is a not unreasonable place to expect to find it, in the circumstances, given the woman's mentality. We'd better inspect it as soon as possible. It will be guarded by now, of course.'

'You can fix the guards?' Disraeli asked.

'Of course,' Palmerston said.

'How about shooting a bit of hardware through the hole?'

They all consulted. The general feeling was that since they and possibly the whole world were doomed anyway, they might as well try a few H-bombs.

'No!' Utrect said. 'Listen, think out the situation, gentlemen! We all have to accept the truth now. At last it is in the open. Our world, as we believed we knew it, is a fake, a fake almost from top to bottom. Everything we accept as a natural factor is a deception, mocked-up by someone – or some civilisation – of almost unbelievable technological ability. Can you imagine the sheer complexity of a mind that invented human history alone? Pilgrim Fathers? Ice Age? Thirty Years War?? Charlemagne? Ancient Greece? The Albigensians? Imperial Rome? Abe Lincoln? The Civil War? All a tissue of lies – woven, maybe, by poly-progged computers.

'Okay. Then we have to ask *why*? What did they go to all the trouble for? Not just for fun! For an experiment of some kind. In some way, we must be a benefit to them. If we could see what that benefit was, then we might be in a bargaining position with – Queen Victoria.'

There was a moment of silence.

'He has a point,' Dickens said.

'We've no time,' Disraeli said. 'We want action. I'll settle for bombs.'

106

'No, Disraeli,' Albert said. 'Florence Nightingale is right. We have everything to lose by hasty action. Victoria – or the Victorians – could wipe us out if they wanted. We must bargain if possible, as Nightingale says. The question is, what have we got that they need?'

Everyone started talking at once. Finally, Ruskin, who had the face of a well-known Russian statesman, said, 'We know the answer to that. We have the anti-gravitational shield that is the latest Russo-American technological development. Next month, we activate it with full publicity, and shield the Earth from the moon's harmful tidal action. The shield is the greatest flowering of our terrestrial technology. It would be invaluable even to these Victorians.'

This brought a general buzz of agreement.

Utrect alone seemed unconvinced. Surely anyone who had set up a planet as an experimental environment would already have full command of gravitational effects. He said, doubtfully, 'I think that psycho-analysts like myself can produce evidence to show that the Victorians' experiment is in any case nearly over. After all, experiments are generally run or financed only for a limited time. Our time's almost up.'

'Very well, then,' said Ruskin. 'Then our anti-gravitational screen is the climax of the experiment. We hold on to it and we parley with the Victorians.'

It seemed that the PINCS committee members would adopt this plan. Disraeli, Utrect, and Hoggart were to fly to Britain, meet Palmerston there, and put it into action. The three of them snatched a quick meal while the rest of the committee continued its discussion. Hoggart took a shower and a Draculin.

'Guess you were right to adopt a more gentle approach to Victoria,' Disraeli told Utrect. 'I'm just a dog-rough army man myself, but I can take a hint. We can't expect to kill her. She's safe in her own dimension.'

'I feel no animosity towards Victoria,' Utrect said. 'We

still survive, don't we? Perhaps it is not her intention to kill us.'

'You're changing your mind, aren't you?' Hoggart said.

'Could be. You and I are still alive, Bob! Maybe the object of the experiment was to see if we could work out the truth for ourselves. If we are actually of a primitive cave-dwelling race, maybe we've now proved ourselves worthy of Victoria's assistance. She just could be kind and gentle.'

The other two laughed, but Utrect said, 'I'd like to meet her. And I have an idea how we can get in contact with her – an idea I got from some rats. Let me draw you a sketch, Disraeli, and then your engineers can rig it for us in a couple of hours.'

Disraeli looked strangely at him. 'Rats? You get ideas off rats?'

'Plenty.' And then he started trembling again. Could Victoria really be kind when she had them all in a vast rat-educator, or did he just *hope* she was, for his own and Karen's sake?

When Disraeli was studying the sketch Utrect made, Hoggart said confidentially in the latter's ear, 'This Disraeli and all the other committee members – you don't see anything funny about them?'

'Funny? In what way?'

'They are real people, aren't they, I suppose? I mean they couldn't be dummies, animated dummies, could they?' He looked at Utrect very chill and frightened.

Utrect threw back his head and laughed. 'Come on, Bob! You're suggesting that Queen Victoria could have some sort of power over our minds to deceive us utterly – so that, for instance, when we get to England we shall not really have left the States at all! So that these people are just dummies and this is all some sort of paranoid episode without objective reality! Absolute nonsense!'

'It didn't happen. It was a phantasm of my tired over-crowded brain, without objective reality. Senior members

108

of my staff do not spy on each other.'

Thus spake Prestige Normandi, Controller of the Advanced Alienation Hospital, to himself, as he strode away from Froding's room down the crowded corridor towards his office. He was trying not to believe that Froding really had a bug ray on Utrect; it was against all ethics.

Yet what were ethics? It was only by slowly jettisoning them and other principles that people could live in such densities as Central New York; something had to give; their rather stuffy fathers back in the sixties would have found this city uninhabitable. Under the sheer psychic pressure of population, what was an odd hallucination now and again?

A case in point. The woman coming towards him along the corridor. That regal air, those grand old-fashioned clothes. . . . Normandi had a distinct impression that this was some old-time sovereign, Queen Victoria or the Empress Elizabeth of Austria. He wasn't well up in history. She sailed by, seemed to shoot him a significant glance, and was gone.

Impressed, he thought, 'She really might have been there. Maybe it was a nurse going off duty, member of some odd society or other' – Normandi disapproved of all these societies, believing they tended to encourage fantasies and neuroses, and was himself President of the Society for the Suppression of Societies. All the same, he was impressed enough by the regal apparition to pause at Burton's cell; Burton would know what to think, it was in his line.

But he was too tired for the Freud act. With his hand on the door knob, he paused; then he turned away and pushed through the mob which always jostled along the corridor, towards his own little haven.

Safely there, he sat at his desk and rested his eyes for a minute. Froding was scheming against Utrect. Of course Utrect was probably spying against someone else. It was really deplorable, the state they had come to. Sadly, he slid open a secret drawer in his desk, switched on the

109

power, and clicked switches. Then he sat forward, shading his eyes, to watch the disgusting Froding spying on Utrect.

Utrect and Hoggart were half-comatose, eyes shaded against the bilious light inside the plane as it hurtled eastwards across the Atlantic, England-bound.

The communications equipment Utrect had specified had been built and was stowed in the cargo hatch. Not until they were landing at Londonport in a rainy early afternoon did the news come through. Gripping Utrect's shoulders, Disraeli handed him a message from the PINCS undersea headquarters.

It read: 'Regret to report that the Hiram Bucklefeather Building on Three Hundredth at Fifteenth was obliterated at seven-thirty this morning. All the occupants, estimated at upwards of five thousand, were immediately annihilated. It is certain this was the work of the entity known as Queen Victoria.'

'Your place?' Disraeli asked.

'Yes.' He thought of Karen with her cyanosis and her tragic breathing. He thought of the two unhappy lads, dying a few feet apart. He thought of Cathie, a patient woman. He even recalled the two rats, slaving over their spelling. But above all, he thought of Karen, so keen to seem intellectual, so hopeless at being anything, her very psyche sapped by the pulsating life about her. He had always done too little for her. He closed his eyes, too late to trap a tear. His wife, his girl.

Lovely Elizabeth of Austria, murdered needlessly on a deserted quay beside her lady-in-waiting – an irrelevant tableau slipping in to perplex his grief. All sweet things dying.

As they hurried across the wet runway, Hoggart said shakily, 'Victoria was after *me*, the bitch! She's a bitch! A bloody cow of a bitch, Douglas! Think of it – think of the way she built herself into the experiment as a sort of mother figure! Queen of England – sixty glorious years.

Empress of India. She even named the age after herself. The Victorian Age. God Almighty! Began the experiment with her own supposed funeral, just for a laugh! What a cosmic bitch! By God . . . ' He choked on his own anger.

Palmerston was there to meet them in a military car. He shook Utrect's hand. He had heard the news. 'You have my deepest sympathy.'

'Why did she – what I can't understand – why did she destroy the building five hours after we had left?' Utrect asked painfully, as they whizzed from the airport, their apparatus stowed in the back of the car.

'I've worked that out,' Hoggart said. 'She missed me by an hour at Windsor, didn't she? It's British Summer Time here – the clocks go forward an hour. In New York, she missed us by five hours. She can't be all-knowing! She's going by Greenwich Mean Time. If she'd gone by local time, she'd have nailed us dead on both occasions.'

'Ingenious,' Disraeli admitted. 'But if she can see us, then how could she make such a mistake?'

'I told you I thought there might be different dimensions down this hole we are going to investigate. Obviously, *time* is a little scrambled as well as the space between her world and ours, and it doesn't help her to be as effective as otherwise she might be. That could work to our advantage again.'

'God knows, we need every advantage we can get,' Palmerston said.

Alone in his little office, Controller Prestige Normandi sat shading his eyes and suffering the crowded woes of the world, but always watching his tiny secret screen, on which Dr Froding, in his room, sat scanning the exploits of Utrect on his tiny screen. Psychic overcrowding with a vengeance, the Controller thought; and all the events that Utrect was now undergoing: were they real or, as Froding claimed, a paranoid episode without objective reality, enacted by dummies? Froding crouched motion-

111

less, watching in his chair; Normandi did the same.

A knock at the door.

Quickly sliding the spy screen away in the secret door of his desk, Normandi rapped out an official order to enter. Froding stepped in, closing the door behind him.

Suddenly atremble, Normandi clutched his throat. 'Good Dimpsey! You're not really there, Froding, you're just a paranoid delusion! I must get away for a few days' rest! I know you're really down in your room, watching Utrect, sitting comfortably in your chair.'

Swelling two inches all around, Froding stamped his foot. 'I will not be referred to as a paranoid delusion, Controller! That is a dummy sitting in my chair; it has taken over and will not leave when asked. So I have wrung from you a confession that you spy on your staff! You have not heard the end of this, by any means, nor even the beginning.'

'Let's be reasonable, Froding. Have a calmer with me.' Hurriedly, Normandi went to a secret cupboard and brought out pills and a jug of chlorinated water. 'We are reasonable men; let us discuss the situation reasonably. It boils down to the old question of what is reality, does it not? As I see it, improved means of communication have paradoxically taken mankind further from reality. We are all so near to each other that we seek to keep apart by interposing electronic circuits between us. Only psychic messages get through, but those we still prefer not to recognise officially. Can I believe anything I see Utrect doing when he is removed from me by so many scientifico-artistic systems? The trouble is, our minds identify tele-vision, even at its best, with the phantasms of inner vision – wait! I must write a paper on the subject!' He picked up a laserpen and scrawled a note on his writing-screen. 'So, contemporary history, which we experience through all these scientific-artistic media, becomes as much a vehicle for fantasy as does past history, which comes filtered through the medium of past-time. What's real, Froding, tell me that, what is real?'

'Which reminds me,' Froding said coldly. 'I came in to tell you that Burton/Freud has escaped within the last few minutes.'

'We can't let him get away! He's our star patient, nets us a fortune on the weekly "Find the Mind" show!'

'I feel he is better free. We cannot help him at Lexington.'

'He's *safer* confined in here.'

Froding raised an eyebrow loaded with irony. 'You think so?'

'How did he get away?'

'His nurse Phyllis again, poor Phyllis. He attacked her, tied her up, and left his cell disguised as a woman, some say as Queen Victoria.'

Effortlessly, Normandi made anti-life noises with his throat. 'I saw her – him. She – he – passed me in the corridor. He – she shot me a significant glance, as the writer says. . . . What are we to do?'

'You're the Controller. . . . ' But not for so much longer, Froding thought. Events were rolling triumphantly in his direction. Utrect was as good as defeated; now Normandi also was on his way out. All he had to do now was to get rid of that damned dummy sitting in his armchair.

Undisturbed by the gale of psychic distortion blowing about him, the dummy sat comfortably in Dr Froding's chair and stared at the 3V screen.

In it, he could see Palmerston's large military car slowing as it reached the outskirts of Windsor. The pale face of Utrect looked out at the military barriers and machine-gun posts.

Inwardly, Utrect fermented with anger at the thought of what had happened to his wife. All the hate in his unsettled nature seemed to boil to the surface. He had claimed that Victoria might be kind! He had spoken up against throwing bombs at her! Now he wished he could throw one himself.

Gradually, his emotionalism turned into something more chilly. He recalled the way poor insane Burton was lapsing back into nineteenth-century dreams. He knew thousands of similar cases in New York alone. And all the little secret societies that covered America – they could be interpreted as a regression towards primitivism, as if a long hypnosis were wearing off. He recalled what they had said earlier: the big experiment was coming to an end. The various illusions were breaking up, becoming thin, transparent. Hence the widespread madness – to which, he realised bitterly, he was far from immune. He had enjoyed too deeply pretending to be the Emperor Franz Josef; now his real-life Elizabeth had also been randomly assassinated.

So what was the aim of it all? Timed to run just a hundred years, only a few more weeks to go, this ghastly experiment of Victoria's had been aimed to prove *what*?

He could not believe that all mankind was set down on this temporary Earth merely to develop the Russo-American anti-gravitational shield. Victoria could have got away with a simpler, cheaper environmental cage than this, had she just required the development of the shield. No, the point of it all had to be something that would explain the great complexity of the teeming terrestrial races, with all their varying degrees of accomplishment and different psychologies.

They were slogging across the wet and blasted ground of Windsor now, with two assistants dragging the communications equipment. Utrect stopped short. He had the answer!

It went through him like toothache. He pictured the rats again. Man had carried out simple population-density experiments with rats as long ago as the nineteen-fifties. Those rats had been given food, water, sunlight, building material, and an environment which, initially at least, had been ideal. Then they had been left without external interference to breed and suffer the maladies resulting from subsequent over-population.

114 .

Now the experiment was being repeated – on a human scale!

It was the human population explosion – the explosion that mankind, try as it might, had never been able to control – which was being studied. Now it was breaking up because Victoria had all the data she needed. He figured that lethal interstellar gas would enfold Earth on New Year's Day 2001, a few weeks from now. Project X terminated successfully.

Unless . . .

The assistants were fixing up the communicator so that it shone down the hole. Soldiers were running up with a generator. A respectful distance away, tanks formed a perimeter, their snouts pointing inwards. Each tank had a military figure standing on it, binoculars focused on the central group. A whirler hovered just above them, 3V cameras going. The rain fell sharply, bubbling into the pulverised ground.

Utrect knew what happened to rats at the end of an experiment. They never lived to a ripe old age. They were gassed or poisoned. He knew, too, where the rats came from. He had a vision of the true mankind – primitive people, on a primitive planet, scuttling like rats for shelter in their caves while the – the Victorians, the super-race, the giants, the merciless ones, the gods and goddesses, hunted them, picked them up squealing, conditioned them, dropped them into the big educator. To breed and suffer. As Karen had suffered.

Now, Disraeli and Palmerston gave the signal. Lights blazed along the facets of the communicator. Their message flashed down into the hole, one sentence changed into another and back, over and over, as the letter-drums rolled.

IRECOGNISEYOU

QUEENVICTORIA

OFFERIDENTITY

CONSIDERPEACE

The rats were trying to parley!

115

For the first time, Utrect stared down into the hole that had once been hidden by the mausoleum – Earth's navel, as Palmerston had put it. The light coming from it was confusing. Not exactly too bright. Not exactly too dim. Just – wrong. Nastily and disturbingly wrong. And – yes, he swore it, something was moving down there. Where there had been emptiness, a confused shadow moved. The bitch goddess was coming to investigate!

Utrect still had his flick-knife. He did not decide what to do; he simply started doing it. The others were too late to hold him back. He was deaf to Hoggart's shout of warning. Avoiding the signalling device, he ran forward and dived head first into the dimension hole.

It was a colour he had not met before. A scent in his nostrils unknown. An air fresher, sharper, than any he had ever breathed. All reality had gone, except the precious reality of the blade in his hand. He seemed to be falling upwards.

His conditioning dropped away, was ripped from his brain. He recalled then the simple and frightened peoples of the caves, living in community with some other animals, dependent mainly on the reindeer for their simple needs. There had not been many of them, comparatively speaking.

And the terrible lords of the starry mountains! Yes, he recalled them too, recalled them as being enemies whispered of in childhood before they were ever seen, striding, raying forth terrible beams of compulsion . . . lords of stars and mountains. . . .

The vision cut off as he hit dirt. He was wearing a simple skin. Grit rasped between his toes as he stood upright. He still had his knife. Scrubby bushes round about, a freshness like a chill. Strange cloud formations in a strange sky. *And a presence.*

She was so gigantic that momentarily he had not realised she was there. Of course I'm mad, he told himself. That guy in Vienna – he would say this was the ultimate in mother fixations! Sure enough, she was too big to fight, too horribly big!

She grabbed him up between two immense pudgy fingers. She was imperious, regal, she was Queen Victoria. And she was not amused.

The dummy viewing the scene from Dr Froding's armchair stirred uncomfortably. Some of the things one saw on 3V nowadays were really too alarming to bear.

Dr Froding entered and pointed an accusing finger at the dummy.

'I accuse you of being the real Dr Froding!'

'If I am the real Dr Froding, who are you?'

'I am the real dummy.'

'Let's not argue about such minor matters at a time like this! Something I have just witnessed on the box convinces me that the world, the galaxy, the whole universe as we know it – not to mention New York City – is about to be destroyed by lethal interstellar gas.'

Froding jerked his head. 'That's why I want to be the dummy!'

INTANGIBLES INC.

'Always seems to be eating time in this house,' Mabel said.

She dumped the china salt- and pepper-pots down at Arthur's end of the table and hurried through to the kitchen to get the supper. His eyes followed her admiringly. She was a fine figure of a young girl; not too easy to handle, but a good-looker. Arthur, on the other hand, looked like a young bull; none too bright a bull either.

'Drink it while it's hot,' she said, returning and placing a bowl of soup before him.

Arthur had just picked up his ladle when he noticed a truck had stopped outside in the road. Its bonnet was up and the driver stood with his head under it, doing no more than gazing dreamily at the engine.

Arthur looked at his steaming soup, at Mabel, back out of the window. He scratched his scalp.

'Feller's going to be stranded in the dark in another half-hour,' he said, half to himself.

'Yep, it's nearly time we were putting the lights on,' she said, half to herself.

'I could maybe earn a couple of dollars going to see what was wrong,' he said, changing tack.

' "This is food like money won't buy or time won't improve on", my mother used to say,' Mabel murmured, stirring her bowl without catching his eye.

They had been married only four months, but it had not taken Arthur that long to notice the obliquity of their intentions. Even when they were apparently conversing together, their two thought-streams seemed never quite to converge, let alone touch. But he was a determined young man, not to be put off by irrelevances. He stood up.

'I'll just go see what the trouble seems to be out there,' he said. And as a sop to her culinary pride, he called, as he went through the door, 'Keep that soup warm – I'll be right back!'

Their little bungalow, which stood in its own untidy plot of ground, was a few hundred yards beyond the outskirts of the village of Hapsville. Nothing grew much along the road bar billboards, and the stationary truck added to the desolation. It looked threadbare, patched, and mended, as if it had been travelling the roads long before trains or even stage coaches.

The overalled figure by the engine waited till Arthur was almost up to it before snapping the bonnet down and turning round. He was a small man with spectacles and a long, long face which must have measured all of eighteen inches from crown of skull to point of jaw. In among a mass of crinkles, a likeable expression of melancholy played.

'Got trouble, stranger?' Arthur asked.

'Who hasn't?' His voice, too, sounded a mass of crinkles.

'Anything I can do?' Arthur enquired. 'I work at the garage just down the road in Hapsville.'

'Well,' the crinkled man said, 'I come a long way. I daresay if you pressed me I could put a bowl of steaming soup between me and the night!'

'Your timing sure is good!' Arthur said. 'You better come on in and see what Mabel can do. Then I'll have a look-see at your engine.'

He led the way back to the bungalow. The crinkled man scuffed his feet in the mat, rubbed his spectacles on his dirty overalls, and followed in. He looked about him curiously.

Mabel had worked fast. She'd had time, when she saw through the window that they were coming, to toss their two bowls of soup back into the pan, add water, put the pan back to heat on the stove, and set a clean apron over her dirty one.

'We got a guest here for supper, Mabel,' Arthur said. 'I'll light up the lamp.'

'How d'you do?' Mabel said, putting out her hand to the crinkled man. 'Welcome to our hospitality.'

She said it just right: made it really sound welcoming, yet, by slipping in that big word 'hospitality', let him know she was putting herself out for him. Mabel was educated. So was Arthur, of course. They both read all the papers and magazines. But while Arthur just pored over the scientific or engineering or mechanical bits (those three words all meant the same thing to Mabel), she studied psychological or educational or etiquette articles. If they could have drawn pictures of their idea of the world, Arthur's would have been of a lot of interlocking cogs, Mabel's of a lot of interlocking school marms.

They sat down at the table, the three of them, as soon as the diluted soup warmed, and sipped out of their bowls.

'You often through this way?' Arthur asked his visitor.

'Every so often. I haven't got what you might call a regular route.'

'Just what model is your truck?'

'You're the mechanic down at the garage, eh?'

Thus deflected, Arthur said, 'Why, no, I didn't call myself that – did I? I'm just a hand down there, but I'm learning fast.'

He was about to put the question about the truck again, but Mabel decided it was time she spoke.

'What product do you travel in, sir?' she asked.

The long face wrinkled like tissue paper.

'You can't rightly say I got a product,' he said, leaning forward eagerly with his elbows on the bare table. 'Perhaps you didn't see the sign on my vehicle: "Intangibles, Inc." It's a bit worn now, I guess.'

'So you travel in tangibles, eh?' Arthur said. 'They

121

grow down New Orleans way, don't they? Must be interesting things to market.'

'Dearie me!' exclaimed Mabel crossly, almost blushing. 'Didn't you hear the gentleman properly, Arthur? He said he peddles intangibles. They're not things at all: surely you know that? They're more like – well, like something that isn't there at all.'

She came uncertainly to a halt, looking confused. The little man was there instantly to rescue both of them.

'The sort of intangibles I deal in are there all right,' he said. 'In fact, you might say almost they're the things that govern people's lives. But because you can't see them, people are apt to discount them. They think they can get through life without them, but they can't.'

'Try a sample of this cheese,' Mabel said, piling up their empty bowls. 'You were saying, sir . . . '

The crinkled man accepted a square of cheese and a slab of home-baked bread and said, 'Well, now I'm here, perhaps I could offer you good folks an intangible?'

'We're mighty poor,' Arthur said quickly. 'We only just got married and we think there may be a baby on its way for next spring. We can't afford luxuries, that's the truth.'

'I'm happy to hear about the babe,' the crinkled man said. 'But you understand I don't want money for my goods. I reckon you already gave me an intangible: hospitality; now I ought to give you one.'

'Well, if it's like that . . . ' Arthur said. But he was thinking that this old fellow was getting a bit whimsical and had better be booted out as soon as possible. People were like that: they were either friendly or unfriendly, and unfortunately there were as many ways of being objectionable while being friendly as there were while being unfriendly.

Chewing hard on a piece of crust, the crinkled man turned to Mabel and said, 'Now let us take your own case, and find out which intangibles you require. What is your object in life?'

'She ain't got an object in life,' Arthur said flatly. 'She's married to me now.'

At once Mabel was ready with a sharp retort, but somehow her guest was there first with a much milder one. Shaking his head solemnly at Arthur, he said, 'No, no, I don't quite think you've got the hang of what I mean. Even married people have all sorts of intangibles, ambition and whatnot – and most of them are kept a dead secret.' He turned to look again at Mabel, and his glance was suddenly very penetrating as he continued. 'Some wives, for instance, take it into their pretty heads very early in marriage always to run counter to their husband's wishes. It gets to be their main intangible and you can't shake 'em out of it.'

Mabel said nothing to this, but Arthur stood up angrily. The words had made him more uneasy than he would confess even to himself.

'Don't you go saying things like that about Mabel!' he said in a bull-like voice. 'It's none of your business and it ain't true! Maybe you'd better finish up that bread and go and see anybody don't pinch your truck!'

Mabel was also up.

'Arthur Jones!' she said. 'That's not polite to a guest. He wasn't meaning me personally, so just you sit down and listen to a bit of conversation. It isn't as if we get so much of that!'

Squashed, Arthur sat down. The crinkled man's long, crinkled face regarded him closely, immense compassion in the eyes.

'Didn't mean to be rude,' Arthur muttered. He fiddled awkwardly with the salt-pot.

'That's all right. Intangibles can be difficult things to deal with – politeness, for one. Why, some people never use politeness on account of it's too difficult. The only way is to use will-power with intangibles.' He sighed. 'Will-power certainly is needed. Have you got will-power, young man?'

'Plenty,' Arthur said. The crinkled man seemed unable

123

to understand how irritated he was, which of course made the irritation all the greater. He twiddled the salt-pot at a furious speed.

'And what's your object in life?' persisted the crinkled man.

'Oh, why should you worry?'

'Everyone's happier with an object in life,' the crinkled man said. 'It doesn't do to have time passing without some object in life, otherwise I'd be out of business.'

This sounded to Mabel very like the maxims she read in her magazines, the founts of all wisdom. Pleasure shared is pleasure doubled; a life shared is life immortal. Caring for others is the best way of caring for yourself. Cast your bread upon the waters: even sharks got to live. Mabel was not too happy about this little man in overalls, but obviously he could teach her husband a thing or two.

'Of *course* you got an object in life, honey,' she said.

Honey raised his bovine eyes and looked at her, then lowered them again. A crumpled hand slid across the table and removed that fidgeting salt-pot from his grasp. Arthur had a distinct feeling he was being assailed from all sides.

'Sure, I got objects. . . . Make a bit of money. . . . Raise some children . . . ' he muttered, adding. 'And knock a bit of shape into the yard.'

'Very commendable, very honourable,' the crinkled man said in a warm tone. 'Those are certainly fine objectives for a young man, fine objectives. To cultivate the garden is especially proper. But those, after all, are the sort of objectives everyone has. A man needs some special, private ambition, just to distinguish himself from the herd.'

'I'm never likely to mistake myself for anyone else, mister,' Arthur said unhappily. He could tell by Mabel's silence that she approved of this interrogation. Seizing the pepper-pot, he began to twirl that. 'That yard – always full of chickweed . . . '

'Haven't you got any special, private ambitions of your own?'

Not knowing what to say without sounding stupid, Arthur sat there looking stupid. The crinkled man politely removed the twirling pepper-pot from his hand, and Mabel said with subdued ferocity, 'Well, go on then, don't be ashamed to admit it if you've got no aim in life.'

Arthur scraped back his chair and lumbered up from the table.

'I can't say any more than what I have. I don't reckon there's anything in your cargo for me, mister!'

'On the contrary,' said the crinkled man, his voice losing none of its kindness. 'I have just what you need. For every size of mentality I have a suitable size of intangible.'

'Well, I don't want it,' Arthur said stubbornly. 'I'm happy enough as I am. Don't you get bringing those things in here!'

'Arthur, I don't believe you've taken in a word this – '

'You keep out of this!' Arthur told her, wagging a finger at her. 'All I know is, this travelling gentleman's trying to put something over on me, and you're helping him.'

They confronted each other, the crinkled man sitting nursing the two pots and looking at the husband and wife judiciously. Mabel's expression changed from one of rebellion to anguish; she put her hand to her stomach.

'The baby's hurting me,' she said.

In an instant Arthur was round the table, his arms about her, consoling her, penitent. But when she peeped once at the crinkled man, he was watching her hard, and his eyes held that penetrating quality again. Arthur also caught the glance and misinterpreting it, asked guiltily, 'Do you reckon I ought to get a doctor?'

'It would be a waste of money,' the crinkled man said.

This obviously relieved Arthur, but he felt bound to

125

say, 'They do say Doc Smallpiece is a good doctor.'

'Maybe,' said the crinkled man. 'But doctors are no use against intangibles, which is what you're dealing with here. . . . Ah, a human soul is a wonderful intricate place! Funny thing is, it could do so much but it's in such a conflict it can do so little.'

But Arthur was feeling strong again now that he was touching Mabel.

'Go on, you pessimistic character,' he scoffed. 'Mabel and me're going to do a lot of things in our life.'

The crinkled man shook his head and looked ineffably sad. For a moment they thought he would cry.

'That's the whole trouble,' he said. 'You're not. You're going to do nothing thousands of people aren't doing exactly the same at exactly the same time. Too many intangibles are against you. You can't pull in one direction alone for five minutes, never mind pulling together.'

Arthur banged his fist on the table.

'That ain't true, and you can get to hell out of here! I can do anything I want. I got will-power!'

'Very well.'

Now the crinkled man also stood up, pushing his chair aside. He picked up the pepper- and salt-pots and plonked them side by side, not quite touching, on the edge of the table.

'Here's a little test for you,' he said. His voice, though still unraised, was curiously impressive. 'I put these two pots here. How long could you keep them here, without moving them, without touching them at all, in exactly that same place?'

For just a moment, Arthur hesitated as if grappling with the perspectives of time.

'As long as I liked,' he said stubbornly.

'No, you couldn't,' the visitor contradicted.

'Course I could! This is my place, I do what I like in it. It's a fool thing to want to do, but I could keep them pots there a whole year if need be!'

'Ah, I see! You'd use your *will-power* to keep them there, eh?'

'Why not?' Arthur asked. 'I got plenty of will-power, and what's more I'm going to fix the yard and grow beans and things.'

The long face swung to and fro, the shoulders shrugged.

'You can't test will-power like that. Will-power is something that should last a lifetime. You're not enough of an individualist to have that kind of will-power, are you now?'

'Want to bet on that?' Arthur asked.

'Certainly.'

'Right. Then I'll bet you I can keep those pots untouched on that table for a lifetime – my lifetime!'

The crinkled man laughed. He took a pipe out of his pocket and commenced to light it. They heard spittle pop in its stem.

'I won't take on any such wager, son,' he said, 'because I know you'd never do it and then you'd be disappointed with yourself. You see, a little thing like you propose is not so simple; you'd run up against all those intangibles in the soul I was talking about.'

'To hell with them!' Arthur exploded. His blood was now thoroughly up. 'I'm telling you I could do it.'

'And I'm telling you you couldn't. Because why? Because in maybe two, maybe five, say maybe ten years, you'd suddenly say to yourself, "It's not worth the bother – I give up." Or you'd say, "Why should I be bound by what I said when I was young and foolish?" or a friend would come in and accidentally knock the pots off the table; or your kids would grow up and take the pots; or your house would burn down; or something else. I tell you it's impossible to do even a simple thing with all the intangibles stacked against you. They and the pots would beat you.'

'He's quite right,' Mabel agreed. 'It's a silly thing to do and you couldn't do it.'

And that was what settled it.

Arthur rammed his fists deep down into his pockets and stood over the two pots.

'I bet you these pots will stay here, untouched, all my life,' he said. 'Take it or leave it.'

'You can't – ' Mabel began, but the crinkled man silenced her with a gesture and turned to Arthur.

'Good,' he said. 'I shall pop in occasionally – if I may – to see how things are going. And in exchange I give – I have already given – you one of my best intangibles: an objective in life.'

He paused for Arthur to speak, but the young man only continued to stare down at the pots as if hypnotised.

It was Mabel who asked, 'And what is his objective in life?'

As he turned towards the door, the crinkled man gave a light laugh, not exactly pleasant, not exactly cruel.

'Why, guarding those pots,' he said. 'See you, children!'

Several days elapsed before they realised that he went out and drove straight away without any further trouble from his ancient truck.

At first Mabel and Arthur argued violently over the pots. The arguments were one-sided, since Mabel had only to put her hand on her stomach to win them. She tried to show him how stupid the bet was; sometimes he would admit this, sometimes not. She tried to show him how unimportant it all was; but that he would never admit. The crinkled man had bored right through Arthur's obtuseness and anger and touched a vital spot.

Before she realised this, Mabel did her best to get Arthur to remove the pots from the table. Afterwards, she fell silent. She tried to wait in patience, to continue life as if nothing had happened.

Then it was Arthur's turn to argue against the pots. They changed sides as easily as if they had been engaged in a strange dance. Which they were.

128

'Why should we put up with the nuisance of them?' he asked her. 'He was only a garrulous old man making a fool of us.'

'You know you wouldn't feel right if you did move the pots – not yet anyhow. It's a matter of psychology.'

'I told you it was a trick,' growled Arthur, who had a poor opinion of the things his wife read about.

'Besides, the pots don't get in your way,' Mabel said, changing her line of defence. 'I'm about the place more than you and they don't really worry me, standing there.'

'I think about them all the while when I'm down at the pumps,' he said.

'You'd think more about them if you moved them. Leave them just a few more days.'

He stood glowering at the two little china pots. Slowly he raised a hand to skitter them off the table and across the room. Then he turned away instead, and mooched into the yard. Tomorrow, he'd get up real early and start on all that blamed chickweed.

The next stage was that neither of them spoke about the pots. By mutual consent they avoided the subject and Mabel dusted round the pots. Yet the subject was not dropped. It was like an icy draught between them. An intangible.

Two years passed before the antediluvian vehicle drove through Hapsville again. The day was Arthur's twenty-fourth birthday, and once more it was evening as the overalled figure with the long skull walked up to the door.

'If he gets funny about those pots, I swear I'll throw them right in his face,' Arthur said. It was the first time either of them had mentioned the pots for months.

'You'd better come in,' Mabel said to the crinkled old man, looking him up and down.

He smiled disarmingly, charmingly, and thanked her, but hovered where he was, on the step. As he caught sight of Arthur, his spectacles shone, every wrinkle animated itself over the surface of his face. He read so easily in Arthur's expression just what he wanted to know that he did not even have to look over their shoulders at the table for confirmation.

'I won't stop,' he said. 'Just passing through and thought I'd drop this in.'

He fished a small wooden doll out of a pocket and dangled it before them. The doll had pretty round painted light blue eyes.

'A present for your little daughter,' he said, thrusting it towards Mabel.

Mabel had the toy in her hand before she asked in sudden astonishment, 'How did you guess it was a girl we got?'

'I saw a frock drying on the line as I came up the path,' he said. 'Good night! See you!'

They stood there watching the little truck drive off and vanish up the road. Both fought to conceal their disappointment over the brevity of the meeting.

'At least he didn't come in and rile you with his clever talk,' Mabel said.

'I *wanted* him to come in,' Arthur said petulantly. 'I wanted him to see we'd got the pots just where he left them, plumb on the table edge.'

'You were rude to him last time.'

'Why didn't you make him come in?'

'Last time you didn't want him in, this time you do! Really, Arthur, you're a hard man to please. I reckon you're most happy when you're unhappy. You're your own worst enemy?'

He swore at her. They began to argue more violently, until Mabel clapped a hand to her stomach and assumed a pained look.

This time it was a boy. They called him Mike and he grew into a little fiend. Nothing was safe from him. Arthur had to nail four walls of wood round the salt- and pepper-pots to keep them unmolested; as he told Mabel, it wasn't as if it was a valuable table.

'For crying aloud, a grown man like you!' she exclaimed impatiently. 'Throw away those pots at once! They're getting a regular superstition with you. And when are you going to do something about the yard?'

He stared darkly and belligerently at her until she turned away.

Mike was almost ten years old, and away bird-snaring in the woods, before the crinkled man called again. He arrived just as Arthur was setting out for the garage one morning, and smiled engagingly as Mabel ushered him into the front room. Even his worn old overalls looked unchanged.

'There are your two pots, mister,' Arthur said proudly, with a gesture at the table. 'Never been touched since you set 'em down there, all them years ago!'

Sure enough, there the pots stood, upright as sentries.

'Very good, very good!' the crinkled man said, looking really delighted. He pulled out a notebook and made an entry. 'Just like to keep a note on all my customers,' he told them apologetically.

'You mean to say you've folks everywhere guarding salt-pots?' Mabel asked, fidgeting because she could hear the two-year-old crying out in the yard.

'Oh, they don't only guard salt-pots,' the crinkled man said. 'Some of them spend their lives collecting match-box tops, or sticking little stamps in albums, or writing words in books, or hoarding coins, or running other people's lives. Sometimes I help them, sometimes they manage on their own. I can see you two are doing fine.'

'It's been a great nuisance keeping the pots just so,' Mabel said. 'A man can't tell how much nuisance.'

The crinkled man turned on to her that penetrating look she remembered so well, but said nothing. Instead, he switched to Arthur and enquired how work at the garage was going.

'I'm head mechanic now,' Arthur said, not without pride. 'And Hapsville's growing into a big place now – yes, sir! New canning factory and everything going up. We've got all the work we can handle at the garage.'

'You're doing fine,' the crinkled man assured him again. 'But I'll be back to see you soon.'

Soon was fourteen years.

The battered old vehicle with its scarcely distinguishable sign drew up in front of the bungalow and the crinkled man climbed out. He looked about with interest. Since his last visit, Hapsville had crawled out to Arthur's place and embraced it with neat little wooden doll's houses on either side of the highway. Arthur's place itself had changed. A big new room was tacked on to one side; the whole outside had been recently repainted; a lawn with rose bushes fringing it lapped up to the front fence. No sign of chickweed.

'They're doing O.K.,' the crinkled man said, and went and knocked on the door.

A young lady of sixteen greeted him, and guessed at once who he was.

'My name's Jennifer, and I'm sixteen and I've been looking forward to seeing you for simply ages! And you'd better come on in because Mom's out in the yard doing washing, and you can come and see the pots because they're just in the same place and never once been moved. Father says it's a million years' bad luck if we touch them, 'cause they're intangible.'

Chattering away, she led the crinkled man into the old room. It too had changed; a bed stood in it now and several faded photographs hung on the wall. An old man with a face as pink as sunset sat in a rocking-chair and nodded contentedly when Jennifer and the crinkled man entered. 'That's Father's Pop,' the girl explained, by way of introduction.

One thing was familiar and unchanged. A bare table stood in its usual place, and on it, near the edge and not quite touching each other, were two little china pots. Jennifer left the crinkled man admiring them while she ran to fetch her mother from the yard.

'Where are the other children?' the crinkled man asked Father's Pop by way of conversation.

'Jennifer's all that's left,' Father's Pop said. 'Prue the eldest, she got married like they all do. That would be before I first came to live here. Six years, most like, maybe seven. She married a miller called Muller. Funny thing that, huh? – A miller called Muller. And they got a little girl called Millie. Now Mike, Arthur's boy, he was a young dog. He was good for nothing but reproducin'. And when there was too many young ladies that should have known better around here expecting babies – why, then young Mike pinches hold of an automobile from his father's garage and drives off to San Diego and joins the Navy, and they never seen him since.'

The crinkled man made a smacking noise with his lips, which suggested that although he disapproved of such carryings on he had heard similar tales before.

'And how's Arthur doing?' he asked.

'Business is thriving. Maybe you didn't know he bought the garage down town last fall? He's the boss now!'

'I haven't been around these parts for nearly fifteen years.'

'Hapsville's going up in the world,' Father's Pop murmured. 'Of course, that means it ain't such a comfortable place to live in any more. . . . Yes, Arthur bought up the old garage when his boss retired. Clever boy, Arthur – a bit stupid, but clever.'

When Mabel appeared, she was drying her hands on a towel. Like nearly everything else, she had changed. Her last birthday had been her forty-eighth, and the years had thickened her. The spectacles perched on her nose were a tribute to the persistence with which she had tracked down home psychology among the advert columns of her perennial magazines. Experience, like a grindstone, had sharpened her expression.

Nevertheless, she allowed the crinkled man a smile and greeted him cordially enough.

'Arthur's at work,' she said. 'I'll draw you a mug of cider.'

'Thank you kindly,' he said, 'but I must be getting along. Only just called in to see how you were all doing.'

'Oh, the pots are still there,' Mabel said, with a sudden approach to asperity, sweeping her hand towards the pepper and salt. Catching sight as she did so of Jennifer lolling in the doorway, she called, 'Jenny, you get on stacking them apples like I showed you. I want to talk with this gentleman.'

She took a deep breath and turned back to the crinkled man. 'Now,' she said. 'You keep longer and longer intervals between your calls here, mister. I thought you were never going to show up again. We've had a very good offer for this plot of ground, enough money to set us up for life in a better house in a nicer part of town.'

'I'm so glad to hear of it.' The long face crinkled engagingly.

'Oh, you're glad are you?' Mabel said. 'Then let me tell you this: Arthur keeps turning that very good offer down just because of these two pots sitting there. He says if he sells up, the pots will be moved, and he don't like the idea of them being moved. Now what do you say to that, Mister Intangible?'

The crinkled man spread wide his hands and shook his head from side to side. His wrinkles interwove busily.

'Only one thing to say to that,' he told her. 'Now this little bet we made has suddenly become a major inconvenience, it must be squashed. How'll it be if I remove the pots right now before Arthur cames home; then you can explain to him for me, eh?'

He moved over to the table, extending a hand to the pots.

'Wait!' Mabel cried. 'Just let me think a moment before you touch them.'

'Arthur'd never forgive you if you moved them pots,' Father's Pop said from the background.

'It's too much responsibility for me to decide,' Mabel

134

said, furious with herself for her indecision. 'When you think how we guarded them while the kids were small. Why, they've stood there a quarter of a century. . . . '

Something caught in her voice.

'Don't you fret,' the crinkled man consoled her. 'You wait till Arthur's back and then tell him I said to forget all about our little bet. Like I explained to you right back in the first place, it's impossible to do even a simple thing with all the intangibles against you.'

Absent-mindedly, Mabel began to dry her hands on the towel all over again.

'Can't you wait and explain it to him yourself?' she asked. 'He'll be back in half an hour for a bite of food.'

'Sorry. My business is booming too – got to go and see a couple of young fellows breeding a line of dogs that can't bark. I'll be back along presently.'

And the crinkled man came back to Hapsville as he promised, nineteen years later. There was snow in the air and mush on the ground, and Arthur's place was hard to find. A big cinema showing a film called 'Lovelight' bounded it on one side, while a new six-lane by-pass shuttled automobiles along the other.

'Looks like he never sold out,' the crinkled man commented to himself as he trudged up the path.

He got to the front door, hesitating there and looking round again. The garden, so trim last time, was a wilderness now; the roses had given away to cabbage stumps, old tickets and ice-cream cartons fringed the cinema wall. Chickweed was springing up on the path. The house itself looked a little rickety.

'They'd never hear me knock for all this traffic,' the crinkled man said. 'I better take a peek inside.'

In the room where the china pots still stood, a fire burned, warming an old man in a rocking-chair. He and the intruder peered at each other through the dim air.

'Father's Pop!' the crinkled man exclaimed. For a moment he had thought . . .

135

'What you say?' the old fellow asked. 'Can't hear a thing these days. Come here. . . . Oh, it's you! Mister Intangibles calling in again. Been a durn long while since you were around!'

'All of nineteen years, I guess. Got more folks to visit all the time.'

'What you say? Didn't think to see me still here, eh?' Father's Pop asked. 'Ninety-seven I was last November, ninety-seven. Fit as a fiddle, too, barring this deafness.'

Someone else had entered the room by the rear door. It was a woman of about forty-five, plain, dressed in unbecoming mustard-green. Something bovine in her face identified her as a member of the family.

'Didn't know we had company,' she said. Then she recognised the crinkled man. 'Oh, it's you, is it? What do you want?'

'Let's see,' he said. 'You'd be – why, you must be Prue, the eldest, the one who married the miller!'

'I'll thank you not to mention him,' Prue said sharply. 'We saw the last of him two years ago, and good riddance to him.'

'Is that so? Divorce, eh? Well, it's fashionable, my dear. . . . And your little girl?'

'Millie's married, and so's my son Rex, and both living in better cities than Hapsville,' she told him.

'That so? I hadn't heard of *Rex*.'

'If you want to see my father, he's through here,' Prue said, abruptly, evidently anxious to end the conversation.

She led the way into a bedroom. Here curtains were drawn against the bleakness outside and a bright bedside lamp gave an illusion of cosiness. Arthur, a *Popular Mechanics* on his knees, sat huddled up in bed.

It was thirty-three years since they had seen each other. Arthur was hardly recognisable, until you discovered the old contours of the bull under his heavy jowls. During middle-age he had piled up bulk which he was now losing. His eyebrows were ragged; they all but concealed his eyes, which lit in recognition. His hair was grey and un-combed.

Despite the gulf of years which separated their meeting, Arthur began to talk as if it were only yesterday that they had spoken.

'They're still in there on the table, just as they always were. Have you seen them?' he asked eagerly.

'I saw them. You've certainly got will-power!'

'They never have been touched all these years! How ... how long's that been, mister?'

'Forty-five years, all but.'

'Forty-five years!' Arthur echoed. 'It doesn't seem that long. . . . Shows what an object in life'll do, I suppose. Forty-five years. . . . That's a terrible lot of years, ain't it? You ain't changed much, mister.'

'Keeps a feller young, my job,' the crinkled man said, crinkling.

'We got Prue back here now to help out,' Arthur said, following his own line of thought, 'She's a good girl. She'd get you a bite to eat, if you asked her. Mabel's out.'

The crinkled man polished up his spectacles on his overalls.

'You haven't told me what you're doing lying in bed,' he said gently.

'Oh, I sprained my back down at the garage. Trying to lift a chassis instead of bothering to get a jack. We had a lot of work on hand. I was aiming to save time. Should have known better at my age.'

'How many garages you got now?'

'Just the one. We – I got a lot of competition from big companies, had to sell up the down-town garage. It's a hard trade. Cut-throat. Maybe I should have gone in for something else, but it's too late to think of changing now. . . . Doctor says I can get about again in the spring.'

'How long have you been in bed?' the crinkled man asked.

'Weeks, on and off. First it's better, then it's worse. You know how these things are. I should have known better.

137

These big gasoline companies squeeze the life out of you. . . . Mabel goes down every day to look after the cash for me. Look, about them pots – '

'Last time I came, I told your lady wife to call the whole thing off.'

Arthur plucked peevishly at the bedclothes, his hands shining redly against the grey coverlet. In a moment of pugnacity he looked more his old self.

'You know our bet can't be called off,' he said pettishly. 'Why d'you talk so silly? It's just something I'm stuck with. It's more than my life's worth to think of moving those two pots now. Mabel says it's jinx and that's just about what it is. Move them and anything might happen to us! Life ain't easy and don't I know it.'

The long head wagged sadly from side to side.

'You got it wrong,' the crinkled man said. 'It was just a bet we made one night when we were kind of young and foolish. People get up to the oddest things when they're young. Why, I called on some young fellows just last week, they're trying to launch mice into outer space, if you please!'

'Now you're trying to make me lose the bet!' Arthur said excitedly. 'I never did trust you and your Intangibles too much. Don't think I've forgotten what you said that first time you come here. You said something would make me change my mind, you thought I'd go in there and knock 'em off the table one day. Well – I never have! We've even stuck on in this place because of those two pots, and that's been to our disadvantage.'

'Guess there's nothing I can say, then.'

'Wait! Don't go!' Arthur stretched out a hand, for the crinkled man had moved towards the door. 'There's something I want to ask you.'

'Go ahead.'

'Those two pots – although we never touch 'em, if you look at them you'll see something. You'll see they got no dust on them! Shall I tell you why? It's the traffic vibration from the new by-pass. It jars all the dust off the pots.'

'Useful,' the crinkled man said cautiously.

'But that's not what worries me,' Arthur continued. 'That traffic keeps on getting worse all the time. I'm scared that it will get so bad it'll shake the pots right off the table. They're near the edge, aren't they? They could easily be shaken off, just by all that traffic roaring by. Supposing they are shaken off – does that count?'

He peered up at the crinkled man's face, but lamplight reflecting from his spectacles hid the eyes. There was a long silence which the crinkled man seemed to break only with reluctance.

'You know the answer to that one all the time, Arthur,' he said. It was the only time he ever used the other's name.

'Yep,' Arthur said slowly. 'Reckon I do. If them pots were rattled off the table, it would mean the intangibles had got me.'

Gloomily, he sank back on to the pillows. The *Popular Mechanics* slid unregarded on to the floor. After a moment's hesitation, the crinkled man turned and went to the door; there, he hesitated again.

'Hope you'll be up and about again in the spring,' he said softly.

That made Arthur sit up abruptly, groaning as he did so.

'Come and see me again!' he said. 'You promise you'll be round again?'

'I'll be round,' the crinkled man said.

Sure enough, his antique truck came creaking back into the multiple lanes of Hapsville traffic another twenty-one years later. He turned off the by-pass and pulled up.

'Neighbourhoods certainly do change fast,' he said.

The cinema looked as if it had been shut down for a long time. Now it was evidently used as a furniture warehouse, for a big pantechnicon was loading up divans outside it. Behind Arthur's place, a block of ugly flats stood; children shrieked and yelled down its side alley. On the other side of the busy highway was a row of small stores selling candies and pop records and the like. Behind the stores was a busy helicopter port.

He made his way down a narrow side alley, and there, squeezed behind the rear of the drug store, was Arthur's place. Nature, pushed firmly out elsewhere, had reappeared here. Ivy straggled up the posts of the porch and weeds grew tall enough to look in all the windows. Chickweed crowded the front step.

'What do you want?'

The crinkled man would have jumped if he had been the jumping kind. His challenger was standing in the half-open doorway, smoking a pipe. It was a man in late middle-age, a bull-like man with heavy, unshaven jowls and grey streaking his hair.

'Arthur!' the crinkled man exclaimed. And then the other stepped out into a better light to get a closer look at him.

'No, it can't be Arthur,' the crinkled man said. 'You must be – Mike, huh?'

'My name's Mike. What of it?'

'You'd be – sixty-four?'

'What's that to you? Who are you – police? No – wait a bit! I know who you are. How come you arrive here today of all days?'

'Why, I just got round to calling.'

'I see.' Mike paused and spat into the weeds. He was the image of his father, and evidently did not think any faster.

'You're the old pepper and salt guy?' he enquired.

'You might call me that, yes.'

'You better go in and see Ma.' He moved aside reluctantly to let the crinkled man squeeze by.

Inside, the house was cold and damp and musty. Mabel hobbled slowly round the bedroom, putting things into a large, black bag. When the crinkled man entered the room, she came close to him and stared at him, nodding to herself. She herself smelt cold and damp and musty.

She was eighty-eight. Under her threadbare coat, she had shrunken into a little old lady. Her spectacles glinted on a nose still sharp but incredibly frail. But when she spoke her voice was as incisive as ever.

'I thought you'd be here,' she said. 'I said you'd be here. I told them you'd come. You would want to see how it ended, wouldn't you? Well – so you shall. We're selling up. Selling right up. We're going. Prue got married again – another miller, too. And Mike's taking me out to his place – got a little shack in the fruit country, San Diego way.'

'And . . . Arthur?' the crinkled man prompted.

She shot him another hard look.

'As if you didn't know!' she exclaimed, her voice too flinty for tears. 'They buried him this morning. Proper funeral service. I didn't go. I'm too old for any funerals but my own.'

'I wish I'd come before . . . ' he said.

'You come when you think you'll come,' Mabel said, shortly. 'Arthur kept talking about you, right to the last. . . . He never got out of his bed again since that time he bust up his back down at the garage. Twenty-one years he lay in that bed there. . . . '

She led the way into the front room where they had once drunk diluted soup together. It was very dark there now, a sort of green darkness, with the dirty panes and the weeds at the windows. The room was completely empty except for a table with two little china pots standing on it.

The crinkled man made a note in his book and attempted to sound cheerful.

'Arthur won his bet all right! I sure do compliment him,' he said. He walked across the room and stood looking down at the two pots.

'To think they've stood there undisturbed for sixty-six years . . . ' he said.

'That's just what Arthur thought!' Mabel said. 'He never stopped worrying over them. I never told him, but I used to pick them up and dust them every day. A woman's got to keep the place clean. He'd have killed me if he found out, but I just couldn't bear to see him believing in anything so silly. As you once said, women have got their own intangibles, just like men.'

Nodding understandingly, the crinkled man made one final entry in his notebook. Mabel showed him to the door.

'Guess I won't be seeing you again,' he said.

She shook her head at him curtly, for a moment unable to speak. Then she turned into the house, hobbled back into her dark bedroom, and continued to pack up her things.

SINCE THE ASSASSINATION

She had no sensation of falling.

In perfection, she rode the thin air down, her body in a rigidly exultant attitude as she plunged towards the blue American earth, controlling her rate of fall by the slightest movements of neck and head.

In these tranced moments, she almost lost the sense of her own identity. She was pleased to strip off her character, always feeling it inadequate. Because of that, sky-diving had become a consolation then an obsession; she was too remote from herself to be other than remote from her husband, Russell Crompton, Secretary of State. And since the assassination of the President, a month ago, the vast new burdens he had had to shoulder – burdens fore-shadowing the future – had driven them even farther apart.

So every day she flung herself from his private plane, snatching seconds of a rapture immeasurable on terrestrial time scales. I feel now the future in the instant.

Those seconds were compressed with luminous com-prehensions, hard to grasp when the sky-dive was over, when she was confined to earth. In the city one knows not the great hinterland. She understood that a new epoch was about to emerge – on the ground, little men without wisdom sought to deliver it, just as they sought to find the assassin, rating one task no higher than the other. Her husband also hoped to be strong and great on these points but, in her reading of his character, she denied him the ultimate power. She knew a man who had that kind of

143

power: Jacob Byrnes, Jake, hero, victim, clown, seer: and spoke his name secretly into her breathing mask. His thought reaches me.

Her great swoop through the upper air had brought her to 2,250 feet. Now her relationship with the ground was an imminent one, and she pulled at her ripcord to release the first parachute; her equipment was of the simplest, as if she liked to keep this miracle natural.

Below her grew the drop zone, recently created in one corner of the Russell estate. Crompton was richer than Jake Byrnes, the craftier politician too, which was why he had survived where Jake had gone under. Why compare the two? She had Jake on her mind, had a sudden image of him – no, that did not make sense; these images of the future could not always be regarded as precognitive since perhaps more than one kind of time prevailed undetected in the universe: but the image clearly showed her welcoming Jake into his own house. He had been injured in some way but was smiling at her. Curious; in their rare meetings, he seemed not to like her greatly.

Before she landed, square in the target area, she saw Russell was waiting for her, a lonely figure leaning against his black roadster, wearing the simple mack he affected when he was experiencing isolation and wanted to feel like one of the people.

He came towards her frowning, so that she was careful to avoid tumbles and to land on her feet. A last-moment spill of wind took her running towards him; Crompton had to put out a hand to stop her, steadying her by the shoulder.

'Rhoda! I thought I'd find you playing this game. I want you to come on a drive with me.'

He was stern because he disliked this obsession of hers. A Freudian was Crompton, who liked in his relaxed moments to talk the straight jargon and explain grandly to Rhoda that she suffered from the death wish and was 'really' trying to kill herself by this sky-diving. With more

144

oblique views on what was reality, she kept her own counsel; a reserved woman.

She took off her goggles and unzipped her leather suit. He could not but observe her red lips and the fine fair hair suddenly blowing free. A marvellous unreachable woman who irritated him at this moment because she would not ask where he wanted her to go.

'Get a shower and change, will you? I'm going to drive down to Gondwana Hills and consult Jacob Byrnes. I want you to come along.'

Again he waited for her to sneer and ask, 'So that I can defend you from your old flame Miriam Byrnes?' But she never sneered, never said the obvious. Maybe that was what he enjoyed about Miriam and her like; when politics had grown so complex, women should remain simple. Did this one read his thoughts? He looked away, frightened about his own transparency; nervous illness simmered inside him, manifesting itself in disquieting intuitions that others knew evil things about him; he felt himself trapped in a gothic entanglement of questioning. The robust wisdom of Byrnes would act like a salve.

'Is Jacob Byrnes back in favour?' she asked, as he walked with her towards the changing-room.

'They're calling him in this present trouble. If only we could find the killer, get the reporters off our necks, get behind shelter, stop this glare of public scrutiny. . . . I figure it might pay to see him. I want him to meet . . . Never mind that. My office tell me even Vice-President Strawn rang him day before yesterday.'

President Strawn, she thought; the demotion must be meaningful. She shucked off her suit and strode naked into the shower; let him look.

Whatever happened, she too wished to see Byrnes. The image was healthful.

The little dictation machine stood silent for five minutes before ex-Secretary of State Jacob Byrnes, completed his sentence. In that while, Byrnes' heavy and capable mind

145

had hunted over a wide range of topics past and present, docketing them, methodically cataloguing and compressing them into the inadequacy of words. At last, setting down the cigar, he said ' . . . conclude – *have* to conclude that the present is an epoch in which the new relationship between man and the universe remains, for the reasons above outlined, merely incipient. This is the central factor . . . '

His central factor, at least. This vast memoir, designed in the first place to vindicate his forced retirement from the government and clear away the old scandals of ten years ago, had turned into a philosophical search; personal aspects had been lost, sunk in oceanic thinking. The pauses between sentences, the bouts of research, grew longer, Grigson's fingers above the dictation machine more idle, as Byrnes pressed hotly on, growing nearer to the truth. He knew he was getting nearer; the secret something that prevented a brave new universal relationship forming pressed down on him and on his whole estate here at Gondwana Hills, bringing him churning images, random snatches of possibility.

'What was that, Grigson?'

' "The central factor", sir.' The secretary masterfully obliterated his own personality, crushed by the Byrnes dollars, unable to crystallise into his own potential. Byrnes, who lived by empathy, derived only a blank from the man, and often longed to hit him. He had done so once, when plagued by something Miriam had done. Grigson had taken it well, of course.

'Central factor operating on the collective conscious. A break-through into a higher consciousness has been aborted by the unfavourable cross-currents of mid-twentieth century, resulting in the waking nightmare of inappropriate politico-economic systems imposing themselves all over the globe. The Cold War and the Vietnamese War must be regarded as faulty psychic frameworks through which favourable developments are eclipsed by unfavourable ones.'

Still dictating, he rose and went on to the wide balcony. There was a microphone here; no chance of Grigson not hearing. He liked to stand here and dictate, with the hills in the distance, the private landing-ground and, nearer, the ornamental lake. Nearer still, were the essential adjuncts to the house, such as the gymnasium, his son Marlo's squash court, the stables, and the swimming-pool, which lay against the broad terrace with its statuary. They were laid out in an arrangement that did not please Byrnes, although he had been meticulous with the architect about the matter; but the spatial relationship remained in some way meagre. He lifted up his eyes unto the hills. That at least was okay. Even the line of the toll-road was being erased year by year as the trees grew up. Not that he has so many more years. . . .

Miriam was swimming in the pool. 'Hi!' she called, and he signalled back. There was still communication on the non-resonant level, which maybe counted for something after ten years. She swam in the nude now, her depilated body gold-brown under the water; somehow, he had ceased to worry about the staff looking on. He had even caught Grigson peeping. The tough guys on the guard fence were the most nuisance, but Byrnes had long since conceded to himself that, in view of his wife's feeble mental equilibrium, her need to exhibit herself was better not repressed. Poor little Miriam: however much she stressed the invitation, what she had to offer was pitifully ordinary.

There was more mess around the area than usual. Marlo had some contractors in, an interior décor firm, messing around with something there, some new project. His schizoid son's projects were always a sort of art-therapy; as the search for a self-cure grew more desperate, the projects seemed to grow more elaborate. Byrnes hesitated to intrude on his son's sufferings and saw very little of him nowadays. Bad empathy there. He caught a flickering feeling – one of his images – for a sort of lunar environment, hurriedly repressed an image of his cold first

147

wife, Marlo's mother, Alice. Just as well Miriam saw more of Marlo than he did, although he could not imagine what they said to each other.

Grigson was on the phone. He came out on to the balcony and said, 'Private car at lodge, sir. Russell Crompton, the Secretary of State, wants to speak with you.'

'Let him drive up. Inform Captain Harris in the guard room.'

'Yes, sir.'

The only sort of affirmative statement Grigson ever made. So Russell Crompton was calling. Ever since the President's assassination, his scared successors had been phoning and radioing Byrnes. He was back in favour. It gave him some kind of guarded satisfaction, he realised. But they were all too nervous of bugging and spying to speak out. Now here was Russell Crompton, once a close friend, rolling up at his front gate! There was a nation-wide search for a scapegoat, if not the killer; maybe he'd hear more about that. His particular philosophical beliefs led him to believe that the President's assassin must be a fellow-countryman; the aborted universe-relationship would not allow anything less specific. His stomach churned a little. The more one knew, the less it became!

'No more dictation, Grigson.'

Grigson smiled and nodded, picked up his brief case, and left the room. For a moment, Byrnes lingered on the balcony, surveying the scene which was so shortly to be disturbed. Some things were of such immense value, like the peace of Gondwana Hills and the streams of thought that passed through his own mind; those were of value to him, nourished him, maintained his interest in life, and he hoped that when they were transfixed on to paper they would nourish some other people.

But personal relations also still occupied him. It was a multi-value system in which he enjoyed manoeuvring, in winning and losing points; nor was his enjoyment entirely intellectual. He liked people as he still liked life.

Nor was he too old to feel that he wanted to be seen

148

again at best advantage by Russell Crompton when the
latter arrived. Not as an ageing semi-scholar, a learned
buffoon, but a jolly old political man still able to live it up
as a bit of a playboy. He'd go down to the gym.

And why – he asked himself this as he crossed the room,
taking a last glance at the previous muddle of his creation
– why did he want to act a role with Russell? Russell, for
all his faults and weaknesses, was always direct, never pretended, though he schemed; Byrnes never schemed – well,
there had been occasions – but loved to pretend. But his
playboy role with Russell was almost intended to be seen
through; perhaps the real defence was against Russell's
wife, the rather enigmatic Rhoda.

He wondered what his strong empathic sense would
make of her this sunny day. That sky-diving woman . . .
funny habit for a woman to take up. Beautiful hair.
Something told him she would be accompanying Crompton, unlikely though that seemed.

But he was going to have to talk affairs of state.

Moving in his solid way, making himself more heavy
than he in fact was, Byrnes crossed the corridor, took the
elevator down to ground floor, moved out into the blazing
sun, stripping off his linen jacket as he went. He had a
gun strapped round his waist, being a little afraid of
assassination: or, alternatively, of not being able to kill
himself, should he want to.

'Miriam!' he yelled, crossing by the pool.

'Hi! Coming in, Big Daddy?' She waved a brown arm
languidly to him.

Screw that stupid name! 'Get out and get dressed.
Secretary of State Crompton is on his way up.'

'Oh boy, Fancy Pants! Does he think we're hiding the
Prexy-killer here? Will he want you to run for President?
Is Rhoda coming with him?'

He passed stolidly on, through the ornate stone screens,
imported from Italy and now covered with Russian vine,
and made for the gym, flinging his jacket over a hook, and
working away at press-ups, his face purple. He was a

149

solidly built man on the summer side of fifty-nine and he wasn't going to let Crompton think he was past it. He meditated about his stomach as it touched the floor at regular and straining intervals. The viscera. That was where he felt things. Not a great intellectual man, but a great feeling man. That's what he had been, and almost nobody had guessed – except that bitch Alice, his first wife, who had taken full advantage of it. Even in office, he had to protect himself from the anger of others: it communicated their sickness to him; he was a stable man, wrecked by the storms about him.

You're an oddball, he thought. Few men he could really talk to. But his own company was not disagreeable. Crompton, too, was still by way of being a friend, wasn't he? Strawn too, come to that.

Nose to the ground, he thought of Rhoda again, vexed at himself for doing so. Oh no, Russell would not bring that strange silent creature, surely? But the image told him she was near.

The image took on life. She was standing among bushes; he was very frightened. She was saying, 'We have to cease to rely. . . . ' On what? The image was gone as soon as there. ' . . . on logical systems'; or had he supplied that himself? After all these years, he still did not know how to deal with these moments of insight; which could only mean that his life-pattern had set wrongly long ago; maybe in childhood; he could not take full advantage of the benefits offered by these extra-sensory glimpses.

He stood up, morose. Living was so wonderful, his own faulty faculties were so wonderful; what he needed was a wise man or woman who could discuss such high matters with him. Still in his vest, he moved to the gym door. Crompton's big black Chrysler was just rolling up to the front of the house, Russell himself driving. Rhoda was in the back.

On their way to the bar room, the two men ran through a few preliminary sparring platitudes. The barman mixed them two tumblers of martini and was dismissed.

'I don't know why you want to see me, Russell, but did you have to bring your wife along?'

'Same old grumpy Jacob! You have good nags here and she can go for a gallop. She thought she'd like to see Miriam.'

'Rhoda and Miriam have nothing in common, and you know it. You afraid you've got to keep an eye on her all the while?' He was talking in this vein, he realised, because he was grumpy and had no strong urge to hear Crompton's confidences; the assassination, the troubles of the country, were things over which he had no jurisdiction and which no longer took precedence over his meditative life.

'Why don't you like Rhoda? She likes you.'

He had wanted someone to talk to and here someone was, the Secretary of State, no less. Why not say it straight out, and see what happened, forgetting the fact that Russell was plainly burdened with responsibilities and guilts and worries, and therefore a bad nuisance? 'I am an empath, Russell; I pick up other people's emotions as easily as if I had an antenna on my head. Your wife's eyes always disconcert me. They tell me things I don't want to know, about her and about myself. Look, the future is aborting before our eyes, all the big promises not getting realised; it is creating a barrier of universal mental sickness. Empaths are more sensitive to what's in the air than others. I'm telling you, all our values are false, Russell, false! If –'

'That's what I came to talk to you about,' Crompton said. 'A time louse-up. I agree the priorities are wrong, but I'm in a position to know what the priorities are. A lot of very nasty things have come up this week, things that only the President and one or two men under him knew of.' He took a hefty drink of his martini.

'Things? You mean projects?'

'Sort of. Two in particular. God, Jake, I shouldn't be talking to you about them. They're so secret – well, they are so terrible, that either one of them alters man's relationship to his environment for good and all.'

This came too alarmingly near to the subject of this morning's chapter in the masterwork. Brushing that reflection aside, Byrnes asked, 'Why *are* you talking to me about them, then?'

'I happen to believe that there is a lot of sense in all the philosophical nonsense you talk. I feel I need to hear some of it today. Plus the fact that your barman is one of the world's great artists.'

They stared at each other. It was a hard, tricky world. You had to seek your allies where you could. Although there was some residual evil tinging Crompton's aura, Byrnes said, 'If I can help, I will.'

'We could be bugged here. Let's walk outside.' He swallowed the rest of his drink.

'Bugged? Me, in my own place? The hell with that!'

'I'd feel better outside. I'm claustrophobia-inclined — too many years in Washington.'

Leaving the glasses, they walked through into the sunlight again, through the wide glass doors over which internal steel shutters could close at the touch of a flipswitch. The decorators over in the squash court were making a noise with their machines; otherwise all was silent. The guards lounged in their glass boxes; no birds flew. As the two men walked along the terrace, they caught sight of Miriam and Rhoda riding on ponies towards the hills, Miriam in a turquoise bathing-suit. Why had Miriam been so quick to get Rhoda (or herself) out of the way?

'We'll walk round the lake — if it isn't too far for you.'

'Of course it isn't too far for me,' Byrnes said. 'The years pass more healthily here than in Washington.' He felt his gun uneasily. There was always something about to materialise, sweeping down from the concealed headwaters of the past, deeds already committed in men's minds that manifested themselves like projections from the future; the present was a shock-wave between past and future.

152

When they seemed to him far enough from the house, Crompton started talking. The Administration had been taken by surprise by the death, as if death were an amazing thing. There had not been a strong Vice-President to take over effectively, as Truman and Johnson had done on previous occasions of crisis. Strawn was already proving ineffectual as President. And there had been the secret projects. Some were already almost an open secret among the top men, the usual routinely sinister affairs of the overkill philosophy, such as new missiles and new strains of virus that could incapacitate whole populations. There was a top-secret anti-gravity research station on the. moon, a fleet of interstellar probes a-building in California. But the really burdensome things were none of these. They were two other projects; one had some connection with the anti-gravity moon station, Crompton said. The other was called Project Gunwhale.

'Gunwhale? Gunwhale? What's that?'

'I can't tell you, Jake. I can only say —'

'If you can't tell me, why come here and bring up the subject?'

'The questions it raises are so enormous. Metaphysical questions. Mankind is not ready to face such questions yet. I remember you said something to me once, somehow I remembered the phrase, about "the eternal dichotomy of life". The phrase stuck with me, and it just describes this Gunwhale Project. It seems on the surface to be one of the greatest blessings ever, yet it could easily prove the greatest curse. Its potentiality is so great — no, it can hardly be faced! We shouldn't have to face Gunwhale for at least two more generations.'

'It's something like the A-bomb was in its time?'

'Oh no, nothing like that, nothing.'

Byrnes exploded. 'I don't plan to waste a whole precious day playing guessing games with you, Russell! Either you tell me or you don't tell me! Look, I'm as much a patriot as the next man, but since I was turned out of office, I'm doing my duty by thinking — thinking, goddam

153

it, the hardest job of work there is, thinking for all the guys who never think from one year to the next. Let me get back to my work or else tell me what you've got on your mind and let me help you.'

Crompton was looking back, squinting in the sunlight and staring towards the two figures on horseback, who were cantering now. Casually, he said, 'I back you still, Jake, when your name comes up, so it's only to you I'd say that your temper is the chief of your disqualifications from holding high office. And I wouldn't value the amateur thinking too high if I were you.' He gripped Byrnes' arm. 'You're a good guy, Jake, but you see we are all powerless. . . .'

'Never think it, never say it. Look at this view – man-touched everywhere. God-touched too, maybe, but shaped by man.'

'I can't say anything about Gunwhale, though I'd like to do so. I'll tell you about the other chief headache we're landed with. One or two doctors and psychiatrists know about this, but they are under a security blanket, right under wraps. It's something that happened on the moon. Something that reveals that man's whole conception of the physical world – roughly what we call science – is going to have to be taken to pieces and rebuilt.'

'It's to do with the anti-gravity research you mentioned?'

'Yes, but not in the way you would imagine. It's an effect the moon has on the research staff. Lunar gravity. Christ. . . . Look, I'll give it you straight. For the first time ever, eight men have just spent an appreciable time – six months – on the lunar surface, away from Earth. They were relieved and brought back here last month, four or five days before the President was killed.'

They were hidden from the house now. To afford shelter from the sun, a grove of bamboos had been planted, growing down to the lake, but Crompton walked to avoid these, maybe thinking that they could be bugged. Byrnes stopped by the fishing-pier, wanting to be still and listen as the Secretary of State went on.

'Those eight men are none of them normal any more. The moon has done something to their metabolism; physiologically and psychologically, they are something other than human.'

'I don't get you. You can communicate with them?'

'With the utmost difficulty. To put the whole matter in layman's language – which is all I can understand in this matter – these moonmen are operating slightly ahead of Earthtime.'

'Operating ahead. . . . Living ahead of time?'

'Ahead of Earth time. Earth time is different from lunar time. They figure that each planetary body may have a different time.'

Byrnes gave a laugh of disbelief. 'You should tell that to Einstein.'

'Never mind Einstein! Look, time is in some direct way related to gravity; that's what we've learnt from our eight moonmen. Once you hear it, you shouldn't be too surprised. We've grown accustomed to thinking of Earth as being down a great gravity well; perhaps it's also down a temporal wall.'

'So a time-energy equation is possible.'

Crompton looked startled. 'Nobody told me that. What do you mean, a time-energy equation?'

'Einstein's general theory has been suspect for some while; now his special theory will also have to be re-examined. But if his methods still hold good, then it may be possible to formulate a time-matter-energy relationship. Off the cuff, I'd say this paves the way for the H. G. Wells idea of a time-machine. With computers to help us, a prototype could probably be constructed in a few months. What a vista!'

He stared at the younger man, saw that Crompton was lost, his mind involved in the nebulous machinery of government, not free to speculate, reluctant to make a step that seemed obvious to Byrnes. To get him back into

155

his stride, Byrnes asked, 'How did this temporal effect strike the men involved?' As he put the question, he felt a chill like premonition coming over him, and glanced round, wondering what psychopathic patterns must whirl like furies above the heads of any men so involved with facing the impossible.

'The main effect might not have been noticed for years, but there is a side-effect. Apparently, every living thing including man has built-in cellular clocks which keep pace with the daily revolution of the earth.'

'Circadian rhythms.'

'That's correct. You are better up in it than I am. I get no time for general reading. A long stay on the moon disrupts the cellular clocks. The clocks of this eight-man research team attempted to adjust to the period of a lunar day, which of course was impossible. They clicked over instead into Lunar Automatic, as I've heard it called. They are living .833 recurring seconds ahead of Earth Automatic. The effect now wears off at intervals, as customary gravity brings them back that .833 recurring seconds to terrestrial time. In those intervals, we can communicate with the men. Otherwise, they are schizoid or else seem not to be there at all.'

The orchestra of the inner life ground forth its disharmonies. So the break-through into higher consciousness – the very phrase he had given Grigson that morning – the break-through was now on its way, the possibility of health was again offered, presenting itself paradoxically as sickness! Certain he was being watched, Byrnes swung round, pulling his gun from its holster. Someone was in the bamboo grove, crashing forward. He fired, a reflex of self-preservation. The charging image was a phantom of himself, its mouth open, panting, its heavy old limbs jerking.

As soon as it was glimpsed, it was gone. As soon as Byrnes' shot was fired, the guard car started to roar forward; it sat continually on the landing-field, engine ticking over. In fifteen seconds, the gunmen were piling out by Byrnes' side. Controlling his fury, Byrnes reassured them and set them to searching the bamboo grove. He marched off with Crompton, knowing he would get no more out of the nervous fellow now, ignoring his questioning glance.

'Let me know if there is anything I can do on the moon question.' His voice, he thought, had never sounded so helpless. What warning was that phantasm of the living trying to convey?

'It's essential to know what leading scientists will make of this time division,' Crompton said. He was trembling from the surprise of his friend's shot; the spectre of assassination, hiding still deeper fears, was always by him. 'It's always a question of keeping off the damned reporters. Fetesti has just published a paper on the biochemistries of time; I want to get him in on this. Maybe we could have a top-level meeting with the scientists down here at Gondwana, without drawing too much attention to ourselves.'

'Do that. I'll be glad to help.' He knew it would be dangerous without knowing why. The horrid sensational web of search, treason, and brutality, which always trailed off along its edges into drugs, perversion, lies, and suicide, was spreading once more across the continent; the endemic oppression pattern that sprang from the will-to-power in man's psyche and was always breaking out in new directions; it was the greatest disrupter of a healthful emergent future and could wreck this continent as it had Africa; Byrnes had been caught in its web ten years back; he wished to keep it from Gondwana Hills. 'This whole place is at your disposal. My guard force would be glad of a real job to do.'

'An Interim Committee has been set up. I'll put it to them.' Plainly, that was all Crompton intended to say. Over his averted face fell opaque shadows, as his availability switched to shallower channels, away from the main streams of ego-anxiety.

As they walked back towards the buildings, Marlo came out of the squash court. He was a stringy youth of sixteen, wearing dirty green scandinavian sweater and old jeans. He looked pale and ill. It was the first time Byrnes had seen him for several days. Miriam saw more of him than he did; what they had in common was beyond speculation, but at least she did not shun the child as once she had. But often he disappeared. He had taken to making long journeys, either on horseback or in his own sports car, since he was not certified; and those journeys were as unknown to his father as the fevered excursions of his spirit.

'Marlo any better these days?' Crompton asked and then, as if guessing the answer to that, 'Do you have in a resident psycho-analyst for him presently?'

'It doesn't work for Marlo. The last one tried to cure him with some new drug, and that didn't work either.'

'The boy needs Steicher, a very good man I know in Washington. Steicher would release his repressed ego-aggression.' Crompton believed in all that, but chose not to press the matter, to Byrnes' relief. He had had too much trouble from all the alienists he had engaged to help Marlo; the one before last, a guy from New York, had turned up with two mistresses, sisters.

Marlo hesitated, almost seemed not to notice them, then moved slowly in their direction.

'The death of the President appears to have upset him. On a personal level, he seems to feel little, yet, on the public level, he seems to suffer a good deal. Could he the personality pattern for the future, I guess, unless we solve a few problems. When things get too strong for him, he's completely in retreat.'

'Steicher could help.'

The weight of people in the world, the result of the population explosion, particularly oppressed the boy. Even the square miles of Gondwana seemed not to help things.

'We have to want external aid before it can help us.' He was growing slightly afraid of his son.

158

Crompton said, 'Rhoda said she dreamed about Marlo last night.'

'Yes?' He hardly knew whether it was true.

Making himself smile as Marlo came up, he reached out his hand to the boy, but Marlo slid away, setting his head on one side, with a gesture that seemed faintly derisory.

'They are shooting whales with guns on the lake again, Jacob,' he said. His voice was without animation; his gaze ran through his father. 'Our dear relations, sad to relate The blue whale is now extinct, except in the cerebral seas of the soul, and our lake.'

'What are you having done in the squash court, Marlo?'

As the boy turned on his heel, his eyes just flickered slightly; his father seized on it as a gesture of invitation. Taking a hold of Crompton's arm, to show no malice was borne, he steered him after the boy, who was heading towards the court; the court had been a present for Marlo's fourteenth birthday; Marlo had played only one game of squash there, but had spent many periods living almost entirely in the court, decorating it in various bizarre styles – each of which his psychiatrists had heralded as an advance towards normality.

Byrnes thought of that phrase, 'advance towards normality', now, as he stood with Crompton and gazed at the cluttered interior of the court. The professional decorators had knocked off for lunch, and were eating beer and sandwiches in the upper gallery. Below them, only half completed, was part of a lunar crater, with the star-blotched black of space behind.

Advance towards normality. . . . Just as well he had sacked the psychiatrists, operating like all psychiatrists on false premises; premises such as the notion of a received normality. As Crompton had just revealed, there was a new normality on the moon, where alien time trajectories could taint the human metabolism. And now Marlo was working towards that – like all artists, ahead of his time.

But the moon mock-up was like the sterile territory of death.

He had ceased to ask himself what it meant. But Crompton asked the questions, looking decidedly uneasy.

'Just a coincidence,' Byrnes said. 'The lad's been reading space-comics.' But he had taken a whiff of illness off his son; or had he? Was he not getting whiffs of illness wherever he turned? An hour of crisis was approaching; the higher conscious was about to be born and he stood in the way of its midwives. The boy had disappeared among the builders' junk. He wanted a cigar and another drink.

The two men muttered and walked about and examined the foamed plastic that so closely resembled the seared earth of Earth's satellite, uneasy in the presence of something they could not grasp. As they finally turned to the door, it was to discover their two women framed in the doorway.

'Gosh, are you both okay?' Miriam asked. 'We thought we heard shots, and so we came back to see if anything was wrong. The guards say you saw someone in the grove, Jacob. Is that right? Are there spies around?'

She was almost a head shorter than Rhoda. She kissed Byrnes and gave Crompton a peck as well, as usual meaning nothing she said or did, Byrnes reflected. It could not be said of the alarm she expressed so prettily that it was either real or feigned. 'So long since we saw you, Russ, and I keep telling Rhoda I know you have a great big state secret to tell Jacob, but that's just an excuse and really you came down to see me.'

'You look good in your swim-suit, Miriam,' Crompton said.

'You like it? It cost a packet! Isn't it pretty material?'

Rhoda said nothing. She was terrific in her silence, Byrnes thought; good waves came from her. She was slightly larger than he cared for a woman to be, but her skin and her small, well-shaped breasts . . . well, that was a line of country he no longer found it profitable to pursue; philosophy was at least partly designed to keep that sort of stuff at bay. He went towards her, conscious of how objectional he always behaved towards her. A masked attitude. He suspected she really knew how he felt about her; but if she had that amount of sensibility and perception, then why did he need to put on a performance, like an adolescent? Why did adolescents need to put on performances, come to that? Sometimes whole civilisations became involved in attitudes. The Japanese *haragei*, using attitudes as veils which were only occasionally intended to be impenetrable, saying things that were not meant. The inescapable and gigantic paradox of human behaviour: gigantic, yet so pretty. He wanted to make a note, wanted that more than the cigar or the drink.

He was standing staring at Rhoda. She stared back, entirely without defence or offence.

'Still doing the sky-diving?' Her obsessive hobby was leaping from planes; *Life* had carried an article on her.

'Uh-huh. Still doing the memoir?'

He was still inwardly bothered about the moon thing. Without smiling, he said, 'Maybe I get the same kicks out of philosophy you get out of free fall.'

'You two should compare kicks some time,' Miriam said, shrilly. 'Jacob, take Rhoda in for a cocktail while I show this crazy set-up to Russ.'

'He's seen it.' But he was glad of the excuse. On the whole, he felt women remained private even amid public affairs; it was a vanishing talent. As he led the silent woman away, he sought for ways to shed the *haragei* mask, but she seemed as remote as ever. Almost as if she had more in common with Marlo than with him. It roused his curiosity to visualise her poised in some kind of hallucinatory dream, ten miles above Earth's surface; something of that transfixed state lingered round her still.

'He hates me, you know,' Miriam told Crompton, directly Byrnes and Rhoda had disappeared. 'I cut him off from public affairs in his prime and he can't forget it.'

'He's better away from the in-fighting.'

'Oh, Russ, don't be stodgy with me, please. It's months since I saw you! I know you've got awful troubles with this assassination and all that, but I'm so lonely here. Even Marlo keeps vanishing.'

'Where is the boy?' He was following her over the lunar mock-up.

'He hides behind here. Marlo! Come out, darling! Really, he's getting nuttier than ever.'

Marlo stuck his head out from behind a pillar and said, 'You need to wear a time-suit here. You walk with death. I create my own time and I defy death!'

Miriam looked at Crompton. The words seemed to have struck him a physical blow. 'The boy knows!' he breathed. He turned and walked hurriedly away, out of the court, his hands spread in case he tripped over the equipment lying everywhere.

She followed, calling.

She hung on his arm. 'The Secretary of State scared by a nut-case! He's fun, Marlo's fun! I quite like him.'

'Fun! He's talking about death. . . . And he seems to know about Lunar Automatic.'

She chattered anxiously; he continued to look as if he had seen a ghost, indifferent when she led him in through the side entrance of the house, bustled the maids out of the kitchen, and brought him a beer out of the icebox. He drank with his head down, sighing between draughts.

'You are in a load of trouble or you wouldn't be down here at this time,' Miriam said. 'Tell me about it, Russ. Maybe a silly woman's insight would help.'

'This place is bugged, I'll bet.'

She laughed. 'That's what I'm always saying.' She put her hand over his hairy wrist, but he would not look at her. She slapped him.

'You men are so awful these days, so damned important! Look at me, Russ, am I so ugly now, so old? You used to fancy me. Have you no time for private affairs any longer?'

He switched on the transistor radio set in the counter

and, under cover of the music, said, 'Everything is in chaos back in Washington. Something's happened on the moon – well it's technical and you wouldn't be interested. And another thing. Oh my God! Just before he was shot, the President was going to activate a major project, Project Gunwhale. We've got to decide – more than ordinary guys should have to decide.'

She giggled uncomfortably. 'You don't think you are an ordinary guy. Don't fool with me. You know Jacob treats me with contempt – maybe rightly. Don't you cut me out entirely. . . . One more claim on you, you see! How was Europe, Russ?' He had been out of the country when the President was killed.

'Getting back to New York . . . New York seems so old and incredibly burdened after those young capitals like London and Bonn and Copenhagen. Look, do something for me, Miriam. I don't really go along with these theories of Jake's but he is turning into a wise old man. He's mad, of course, shooting at phantoms, but maybe he has the greatest idea since the cavemen invented fire. Maybe it will now be possible to invent a time-machine. He said something so valuable just now, threw it out. I shall give it equal priority with my other most pressing problems when I get back to Washington.'

'Building a time-machine? I thought that was just a comic book idea!' She laughed. 'Isn't the world complicated enough without going into the future, or whatever you plan to do?'

'Maybe I was already thinking that. Look, all are agreed that right now world affairs have never been more snarled up. Ever since Hitler, nothing but terrible crises: the extermination of European Jewry, Stalin's purges, the H-bomb, the Cold War, Korea, the population explosion, famines everywhere, Communist China. The pressure is not only from the past but from the future, from mouths unborn. Somehow, we have to make a breakthrough before we bog down into universal psychosis. A time-machine could be a way – a marker-buoy sent into future time, to get help or something – I don't know, I'm talking wild.'

'Don't ask me to go into the future!'

For the first time, Crompton smiled at her with real warmth and took her hand. 'That's not what I want you to do for me. I begin to get a sort of superstition. I want you to keep a friendly eye on your step-son, Marlo. Suppose he says anything significant about the moon or time differences, or . . . or people living for hundreds of years, will you note it down precisely and let me know?'

'Doesn't sound the sort of thing I'm good at.' She made eyes at him.

'I don't want your note intercepted. Could you bring it to me in Washington personally?'

She looked soberly at him. 'You do still love me a little, Russ. Of course, I'll do what you ask.'

He stood up. 'Thanks for the beer, Miriam. I'd better collect Rhoda. I have to be back for a conference at twenty hundred hours tonight.'

The newscaster was saying, 'Although the search for the late President's assassin or assassins has recently been stepped up to new levels, official circles in the capital are now admitting that hopes of an arrest are fading. Looks like this is destined to become one of the classic locked-room mysteries of all time. What did happen in the President's study, that evening of 18th August, just before dinner, while the President sat alone, studying – so it's said – an important document which is now rumoured missing? Two of his personal guard sat in the corridor outside, within earshot, yet heard nothing. Here, for a latest opinion on the White House Mystery, is this station's special political correspondent – '

Jacob Byrnes got up and walked out of the room, leaving Miriam sitting on the white velvet sofa, gazing at the screen. Like an invisible presence, Marlo hovered in the shadowed corner of the room. Turning, she called him over sharply and he came, standing a few feet away.

'I have something for you, Marlo. You know what it is, don't you? Your weekly treat. Come nearer.'

He hovered like a bird beyond the patch of lamplight, waiting to be enticed into the hand of its captor. She opened her purse and brought out a screw of paper, opening it so that he could see the cube of sugar it contained.

She gestured towards the TV set. 'For all your funny ways, you dig quite a bit about what goes on in the world, don't you? Washington and Europe, I mean. How's life on the moon?'

He reached out a hand.

'How is life on the moon, Marlo?'

'I am not alone on the moon. Earth is my piece of desolation. Many people live where I live. My mother sent me there, long ago.'

'It's cold on the moon.'

'Cold and hot. More cold, more hot than here.'

'Oh, cut the riddles, Marlo. Do you want this LSD or don't you? What do you mean, many people live on the moon?'

' . . . mounting pressures which were driving the late President into a position of isolation . . . ' said the commentator.

'There had to be a place for unwanted people, or they die of famine or in concentration camps or hospital beds. No room in beds.'

'And the President?' she asked, with sudden intuition.

Marlo shook his head. 'He would have made it all worse. There are too many people already. When the moon is crowded, where do we all go then?'

She gave him the cube of sugar and he retreated with it into the shadows. 'It will do you no good! You're mad already, I suppose you know that?'

'Just ahead of my time,' he said. 'Otherwise there would be nothing. You are nothing. Even when you have all your clothes off, you are nothing.' He put the white cube gently on to his tongue and closed his mouth; and then he stole quietly away.

165

Leaving the TV set to flicker in the empty room, Miriam also got up, and walked down the wide silent corridor, lugubriously lit. Fortunate she believed in re-incarnation; this life sure had its dull moments. At the foot of the stairs, she paused, and then mounted slowly, until she came to her husband's work room. She rapped on the door and entered.

Byrnes was smoking his cigar. He nodded and said, 'Grigson is just sorting some old movies I want to look through. Care to come down to the theatre and see them?'

'Funnies?'

'Not funnies. Sobies. Documentaries or, in your language, dockies.'

'Must you take the piss out of me all the time, Jacob? I came up here for a bit of company.'

He did not answer. He was making notes on a pad while Grigson scuffed in the background.

'You're so busy, Jacob, so dull, shut yourself up here, never even go fishing any more.'

'I went fishing not many weeks ago.'

'That was last summer.'

'So it was last summer, my darling.'

He caught something in her face and said, 'I'm sorry we don't talk more. I must try to produce this old think-piece of mine. I want to finish it by year's end – just the philosophy bit. To hell with the personal stuff; that's forgotten. No time for it.'

'Everyone's obsessed with time.'

'Ask yourself why.'

'Oh, I know all that. Big crisis, big deal! Even Marlo's at it.'

Now he was gathering up the day's notes that Grigson had typed out, absently fumbling a pen to alter and correct and add. ' "Battle between a higher plane of con-sciousness and a waking nightmare that . . . " pretentious, but it will stand. . . . Grigson, have you located that foot-age on the 1934 assassination of King Alexander of Yugo-slavia yet?'

166

'No, sir.'

'Hurry up!'

She stood in front of her husband and said, 'Why are things worse than before? Are they objectively worse? Aren't you just getting old, Jacob?'

'Of course I am getting old! The personal memoir led me into this same question of things getting worse. It's a good question. Do you want a serious answer?'

'No, I just asked for a joke. Me, I'm never serious, am I?'

He caught her wrist as she was about to turn away. 'I'm sorry to tease. I want you, Miriam. I must have some contact with the old world, and you must be it. Listen, I will give you your answer. It's not that things are getting permanently worse; it's just that this is crisis time, what in my book I call "Clock-and-Gun Time". Such crises have occurred before. There was one towards the end of the thirteenth century in Europe, when the towns were growing rapidly, creating new densities. New densities always imply new awareness. Guns and mechanical clocks were then invented, both originating from metalsmiths. Those two inventions brought deliverance from a philosophical impasse and paved the way to renaissance. Guns brought new spatial adventure about the world. Mechanical clocks, incorporating one of the world-changing inventions, the verge-escapement with foliot, were our first precision instrument and directed our inner landscapes towards more precise thinking.

'Those clocks sprang from western society and moulded it. They were no good to the civilised Chinese, whose society had so developed that to them mechanical clocks were little more than toys.

'The same thing may be happening today. Two radical new inventions or discoveries; Russell Crompton mentioned them. They might deliver us. Or they might strike us as no more than toys, marvels. Our imagination could fail before them. We need courage and imagination.'

'That's what your book is going to give people?'

'You see the funny side of me, Miriam. Other people don't, so maybe I can help them.'

She tickled him under the chin. 'Don't do your pathos thing with me. It may have hooked me, but it won't keep me hooked. How is this gun-and-clock talk going to help anyone right now?'

'Isn't it still typical of the dichotomy running right through life? Guns are all externality and violence; clocks are all silence and inwardness. There you epitomise western modes of thought, the ascendant mode on this planet now for several centuries. However bent we are on material things, we never entirely forget our hearts and minds. Okay, now we try at last to join them and reach a new conscious level. Damn it, woman, if the west doesn't do it, who else will?'

'Maybe you have a point there, honey. You are a wise old guy, I do know. Even Russ said so when he was here last week. By the way, I want to drive up to Washington tomorrow, do some shopping.'

'That's why you're being nice to me! Grigson, where the hell is that newsreel?'

Grigson straightened, his face flushed, clutching a plastic spool. 'I have it right here, sir.'

'You're a paragon, Grigson. Miriam – give my love to Russell Crompton if you just happen to run into him, eh?'

Rhoda threw herself from the plane.

Her brain cleared at once. All the irresolutions and obscurities – the poverty of discussion on central things – lifted at once from her mind. At over 20,000 feet, Washington could be seen for the tiny thing it was in both the real and the subterranean affairs of man. And the earth itself; she saw the relationship now, one of magnificent cunning, as a problem that man had posed himself and was about to solve.

She spread herself, arms and legs bent backwards, fixing the world with her mons veneris, adjusting her speed

168

by the subtlest flexion of the spine. From the fifth vertebra spouted ganglia, power, beauty, that charmed the knife-wind. It was the universal nerve centre, counter-pointed only by the blue American earth below.

She wore suit, mask, oxygen cylinder, packed two parachutes. This was her element. Rhoda was high.

There was no sensation of fall, no sensation of fear. Only the beatific equipoise of flight, the collusion with gravity and the forces of the universe, the eternity offered by two minutes of free-fall. She had been on drugs, she had recently tried one of the luxury free-fall holiday schools set up between Earth and Luna, where the very rich experienced psychedelic rapture between planets; but for Rhoda, the true kick came in riding the strato-spheric layer just beyond the realm of her fellow beings.

In this tranced state, she could catch some of the stronger thoughts floating up to her. It always encouraged her to find that only pure or creative thoughts rose this high; the bad ones, of which there were plenty, stayed at around 2,500 feet, just before she pulled the rip-cord. Which was as if the mediaevals had caught a glimpse of that curious scientific fact in their vision of a heaven above and a hell below. Good thoughts breathed hydrogen, the basic substance of the universe. Up here, the all-state manhunt had no being, having no purpose.

She encountered the thoughts of retired Secretary of State Jacob Byrnes; they were rich in hydrogen these days. They penetrated her body. He was troubled. She had no lover. Her husband's thought never touched her here. She had her raptures. She was, she thought, of the future, and so had an interest in seeing it healthily born. Jake was of the past, a dinosaur with love, absurd, heroic. He would die seeing the future enter the world.

This last thought Rhoda examined carefully and languidly as she volplaned down with the world between her thighs. Jake was troubled; he had discovered a sheet of paper. Without understanding what the paper was, she

169

saw its tendrils spread all over the world. She would have to go to help him.

The sky-diving was finishing. She had been aloft immeasurable times, but now a confident circadian clock inside informed her that she was down to 2,250 feet. She needed no altimeter. As she reached inside her leather jacket for the rip-cord, sick thoughts hit her. She caught a whiff of Marlo and knew many things. The parachute was opening; so was her whole area of perception, her mind painfully ripped open to an entirely new level of being, where all was revealed, flaming, frightening. . . .

Her old life on Earth had ended. The plane that dropped her was not her husband's usual sports plane. A parascientific transference had been made; this plane had been – yes, they could not operate tied to Earth, as Wells and the others had supposed – this had been a time-vehicle, winging down out of space on the Byrnes-Fetesti time-energy equation, skimming through the stratosphere, coming as near as it dare to past-Earth, depositing her for this one vital mission to ensure that future was born unaborted.

Yes, from Russell's plane – they had wisely put her under artificial amnesia, but now it cleared – she had been captured from Russell's plane so long ago, carried into the future, trained for this moment, brought back to the point in time from which she had been taken. And the impetus that made it possible for her to come back was the perception by old Jacob Byrnes that the discovery of time-wells along with gravity-wells made time-travel practicable. . . . She admired the symmetry of the design, even as she saw the terror that was to come in the next few hours. Spilling air, the sin-laden air of past-Earth, she sank towards the Drop Zone.

'I wish to resign from my job, sir,' said Grigson. 'It has become anathema to me.'

Byrnes was taken aback. 'You don't like it here?'

'It is simply that you do not like me, sir, and I cannot

170

tolerate it any longer.' He stood rigid in a soldier's posture and had turned very pale.

Byrnes felt an immense shame. He could not face Grigson (what was his first name?); he had to go away, wander like an exile around his own estate. He had treated the man very badly, used his wealth, power, and charisma to purely ill ends, to defeat what little personality Grigson possessed. He had enjoyed doing it. He was an old, bitter, twice-defeated man; even at this moment, his wife, whose life he had blighted, was probably in the bed of one of his successors. No old bull of a herd had ever been so thoroughly routed.

And his son. . . . Had he ever cared that Marlo was isolated, out of touch? With some miserable and ill-defined intent of having a reconciliation with the boy (or at least humiliating himself again?), Byrnes made his way eventually to Marlo's quarters.

It must have been at least two years since he was last in this wing of the building. That told of his neglect! But Marlo was by no means stagnating, whatever else he was doing. He had decorated this whole place, transformed the walls, with some sort of bright plastic stuff, some new material that created an illusory sense of projection, so that it seemed dangerous to walk along the corridor. There were montages too, and meaningless phrases scrawled over the walls and ceilings. WHO KNOWS SPEAKS NOT. NATURAL DENSITY OF LIONS. LIFE REQUIRES MORE LIFE.

Life requires more life. It could be a warm or a cold thought. The appearance of warmth in the new décor might overlie a colder thing: a very frigid horror; such was the image Byrnes derived, although he could admit that the outward semblance was far more cheerful than he had expected. But he paused with his hand on the boy's study door, fearful of opening it, aware only of chill pouring forth at his viscera. Strange images of death. Of course, he was only an old man, failed politician, failed memoirist, failed philosopher . . . but this was not personal death he felt radiating from the room; this was a general death, which included death for the unborn as well as the living. Sick to the stomach, Byrnes opened the door and walked in.

Russell Crompton had his face buried in the warm depilation of her flesh; nevertheless, he could not avoid hearing Miriam say, 'But the guards who were outside the room – the guards must be involved in the murder.'

It was the last thing Crompton wanted to discuss. He said wearily, 'The F.B.I. have virtually taken those two poor guys apart, and they didn't do it, period.'

'Well, what was on this paper that got stolen off the President's desk? Is there a clue there? Was the assassin a foreign spy?'

'Look, honey, if you are fishing for a detective job, forget it. The missing paper is about something called Project Gunwhale – all very hush-hush. It's a top secret memorandum concerning a certain pharmaceutical firm that has discovered a new drug which could change the whole social structure of mankind. If it turns up in the wrong place, wow!'

'Oh, another drug!' She sounded disappointed. This was, she reflected, the third Secretary of State she had lain with; how many girls could claim the same? She answered her own inward question: many more than you'd think, sweetie!

'Christ, I feel flaked out today. That conference on international affairs last night. . . . Many more weeks of this and we won't be able to stand the pace. It's not the work, it's the decision-making that kills you. Man is not a deciding animal.'

'Philosophy I can get at home. Come and lie this way, here. That's better! Tell me about these moonmen. I told you Marlo reckons he lives on the moon. Are your eight moonmen getting any better, because Marlo isn't?'

'You shouldn't feed him LSD, baby.'

'I didn't mean to tell you that, Russ – you'd better forget it. Anyhow, Marlo likes LSD. It brightens him up.

How are your moonmen? Tell me something sensational.'

'Their condition is improving. They still flicker into invisibility occasionally, but that aberration grows less as their circadian rhythms adjust back to Earth Automatic.'

She sat up. 'Invisible? You mean you can't see them?'

'Not the ordinary sort of invisibility. It's just that when they are in the Lunar Automatic phase, they are actually .833 recurring seconds ahead of our time continuum, and consequently cannot be experienced by our senses. Nothing to be scared about, and they'll soon be entirely back to normal, thank God.'

She said, 'I'm not scared; it's just – wait!' But her incoherence did not stop him; after all, men's elaborate affairs, so wonderful if punctuated by the simplicities of bed; he liked the full life, the intriguer within the Administration, liked everything, even the withdrawals of his wife, which gave him moral excuse to diversions like Miriam. He would rise refreshed and encouraged from the seamy bed as from the foam! Already, he was more anxious to talk than to listen, and scheming for possible political advantage from this newly discovered temporal disturbance. He was ready to get up and get back in there pitching, but out of politeness to an old flame he could chat and fondle another ten minutes. Eight, maybe.

'Jake had the inspiration, saw at once that this implies entirely new possibilities for time-harnessing. I phoned Fetesti, who is a head man in the field, apparently, and he's coming to a conference in Washington this evening. A brilliant scientist, they say, Hungarian by origin. I don't want Jake to know I'm meeting Fetesti yet. . . . I really ought to get dressed, pet. If the States could invent a time-machine or a time-projectile ahead of the rest of the world, that would solve most of our problems, huh?' He paused in the act of inserting his right foot in a sock and stared at her pale face. 'You okay?'

'My God, Russ. . . . I told you Marlo was carrying on about living on the moon, and that it was a place for unwanted people to go.'

'Useless, honey. You don't remember exactly what Marlo said. I told you to write it all down. Something half remembered is useless.'

'Okay, okay! But he was talking metaphorically. He didn't mean really on the moon. He meant lunar time.' Suddenly she clung to Crompton, and they nearly fell off the bed together. 'You see – that's why Marlo never seems to be around. He is living in lunar time. He must have been in thought contact with the moonmen when they were carried back to Earth, sick. Their sickness must have corresponded with his. He learnt how to flip that little bit ahead. That's why he hardly ever seems to be around.'

'Marlo time-travelling? Impossible! What was that he said about the President? Try to remember!'

'Something about . . . the President was going to make things worse and there were too many people in the world already. . . . Russ, you don't think it was *Marlo* did it? Not *Marlo*?'

Crompton pulled his pants on, keeping his face blank. 'This is all in your head. It's just ego-aggression on your part, triggered by your guilt feelings because you get that little guy high on lysergic acid. If you could pin the assassination on him, why, you wouldn't have to feel bad at all. I know a good alienist here, guy called Steicher, specialises in repressed ego-aggression. He could help you. Why don't you go and see him?'

She sat very still, staring ahead, not listening, and he noticed with some irritation that she was trembling. 'The locked room – it would present no problem to Marlo if he could move that fraction ahead of time, emerging when he wanted to behind the President. He's acted odd ever since the moonmen came back. . . . He's always away, you can't find him, he goes off in his car, nobody checks where he's been.'

Putting a heavy hand on her shoulder, he said, 'Look, Miriam, granted all that, why would he want to kill the President? What's the motivation?'

Then he remembered: Rhoda had dreamed about

Marlo. He was frightened of Rhoda's dreams; they belonged to some super-reality which even Steicher could not satisfactorily explain away. Rhoda had dreamed that Marlo was playing the name part in a performance of *Macbeth*, which was held in the grounds of Gondwana. The boy had made a great Thane of Cawdor, and had also played the part of the witches, which had much amused his father, Jake Byrnes. Byrnes enjoyed having his house cast as Macbeth's castle, but grew angry when his son insisted on ending the play on the lake, saying that the bamboo grove was moving in to destroy him.

Troubled by the dream, Crompton outlined it to Miriam. To his annoyance, she brushed it aside. 'A dream means nothing; it's the facts that count. Besides, Rhoda's dream has no end.'

'It did end! I remember. She said that Macbeth refused to be killed by Macduff – and the President was playing the part of Macduff!'

'Very cute! And Macbeth killed him instead of him killing Macbeth?'

He shook his head. 'Funny, I remember I asked Rhoda that same question at the time. She did not know. These strange dreams of hers have their blanks. But it ended with Jake running out of the bamboo grove and killing Marlo.'

They stared at each other. Miriam swallowed and said, 'You do think Marlo was the President's assassin, then?'

'There's the motive he wanted to defeat Project Gunwhale, represented in the dream by Macduff's lineage. Its existence was a threat to his life.'

'He had been to the White House as a boy, when his father was in the Administration. Maybe he could recall his way around. But a dream is just a dream.'

'No more, no less. And when I spoke to the boy last week, he said something about shooting whales on the lake. His life is a dream. With the ability to move ahead of time, our precognition becomes for him pre-action.' As he spoke, Crompton felt some of the intense fear Marlo must have done, when looking at the thickening complexity of the future.

It communicated itself to Miriam. She said, 'Russ, is Jake really going to kill Marlo? I'll have to stay here. I'm – I'm scared to go back to Gondwana.'

Mentally disturbed or not, he was again the Secretary of State. Getting into his jacket, he said, 'You believe in the actuality of symbolic levels too, don't you, Miriam? Stay here! But I'm getting down there with some police, fast. The whole nation wants that assassin *alive*.'

She seemed incapable of leaving the bed, was now cuddled down among the sheets, peering at him as he strode across the room as if she no longer recognised him. 'Russ, you don't think that the drugs I've been giving him helped upset him in any way, do you? I really only did it to spite Jake a bit? I never meant . . .'

As he picked up the telephone and began to dial, he said, 'I forgot to tell you, honey. In the dream, you played Lady Macbeth.'

The room was empty. At least, Marlo was not there. It took some while to verify the fact, because the room was so crowded with strange clutter that it baffled Byrnes' sight. He was still fighting the ill-feelings in his stomach.

The boy's sickness, it is anti-life, he told himself. Just because such sickness is prevalent, we must not accept it as normal. It is a rejection. Sickness not the reverse of health but of moral responsibility. . . . People must be warned. Put it in the next chapter. Add that we have to come to terms with the way mental illness functions. After all, it has its own creativity. Illness is a mystery to us. As is health. The nightmares of sleep intrude into waking, and the horrors we face by day walk masked through the night. It's gun-and-clock time, when the orchestration of the inner life falters and the conductor absconds. . . .

The bad images led him to one wall which was covered with recent newspaper clippings, a whole host, secured only along their top edges – the better to rustle and live,

176

maybe – so recent they had not yet had time to yellow. All concerned the murder of the President. Several clips of the famous shot of him slumped over his desk. He had worked till the last, all very touching. You could see the flag behind his chair.

In the middle of the assemblage of fluttering columns was a white sheet of governmental memo paper. Byrnes recognised it at once and read it. He re-read it. On the third reading, it made sense; and its place here also made sense. He clutched his belly.

It was a top secret memorandum addressed to the late President by his advisers, subject Project Gunwhale. It advised that a comparatively obscure pharmaceutical combine, Statechem Inc., had run a three-year test on a new type of gerontotherapeutic drug, patent name Surviva, with conspicuous success on seven species of laboratory animals. No animal showed signs of ageing. Tests had also been carried out on human volunteers in the laboratory staff; although the test period was too brief for any positive results to be expected, all indications were hopeful – no signs of cellular deterioration – grey hair turning black – no deleterious side-effects. Surviva seemed to promise extreme longevity and was inexpensive to produce. Permission was requested for Statechem to ask publicly for volunteers, and for the security blanket on its findings to be lifted. Statechem directors saw no reason why injections for immortality should not be available to all in ten months from the cessation of successful testing.

At the bottom of the memo, one of the President's advisers had written in longhand, 'To go ahead with this in view of present world famines and over-population would shatter all social structures and wreck the planet in one generation.'

Pinned to the memo was another sheet, an answer in what Byrnes recognised as the President's fluid italic script: 'This is an old argument, Ted. If Statechem have it now, someone else will have it soon. We have to okay it and face the problems arising. Besides, we need the addi-

177

tional brain-power: imagine even an extra decade working life from every U.S. scientist. Besides, I'm irrevocably on the side of life.' And his initials, slightly smudged. Must have been the last thing he ever wrote before the killer took him.

I'm irrevocably on the side of life. So am I, Byrnes told himself; can't help it. And immortal life? Well, you'd give it a swing. . . . The resultant problems didn't bear thinking about; and the advisers, perhaps rightly, came out against the idea on that score. But the President, even more rightly, cut them down. . . . Well, was going to cut them down when he was killed. By the initials of the advisers, Byrnes saw that Crompton and Strawn and two other men were involved. They would be no-sayers; and they were the ones now with the power.

And another thing. The killer. This was why he had killed. He would be a no-sayer. Saying no to life, no to the future, no to that terrible tide called progress; you had to say yes and then *do* yes. . . . The killer had killed and come away with this memo.

'Marlo? Where are you?' Marlo would be a no-sayer. His insanity was one of his generation's major ways of saying no. So he had given shelter to the killer, housed the killer here, here in Gondwana Hills. The painful irony of it! The old man felt his eyes burn with tears. His own son sheltering the President's assassin!

He dashed the tears quickly away and pulled out his gun. Maybe the killer was still here. He crammed the incriminating document into his pocket and backed to the door. Wonderfully, the sick feeling had left him. All he felt now was a blind anger, against his son, against the killer, against the circumstances, which he saw were reaching out again to involve him in another disgrace; this one he could not withstand; it would encompass his book, too, overwhelm its frail merits and vital message. The future was dying, the promise of the past collapsing into chaos.

'Come out, you bastards!' he bellowed. The gaudy

tatty room, thugs' hideout, nest of sickness, plotter's par-
lour, den for a murderer, absorbed all sound. It was full
of the dull stained light as associated with sin, a stain he
had seen once in a university production of *Macbeth*.
Light thickens and the crow makes wing to the rooky
wood. It frightened him a little. He backed into the
corridor again, roared his son's name, loud as he could to
bring his courage back.

Marlo appeared before him. One moment he was not
there, the next he was. Although his face was the usual
withdrawn blank, his eyes flared with purpose. He moved
towards his father, ignoring the revolver. Byrnes was
shouting at him, but it was as though neither of them
heard the noise. He got his arm round his father's throat
with a sudden movement and pulled him back, violently,
with an unexpected hard strength. Stars swam in a red
haze before Byrnes' eyes, and his voice croaked off. He
fought, not understanding, the gun still in his hand,
afraid even to hit Marlo with it.

Through the haze, he saw – or dreamed, it felt – Grigson run up, striking out with, of all futile Grigsonish
articles, a leather briefcase. The briefcase caught Marlo
hard under the eye. He at once let go of Byrnes, whimpering. Grigson, looking rather stupid, steadied himself for
another blow; Byrnes sank to the floor, staring pitifully
up. Marlo disappeared: flickered, vanished as if he had
never been.

His senses came back. The idiot Grigson was pouring a
little clear water on his face. Two servants were bending
stupidly over him; there was a third man standing in the
background. Byrnes roared and tried to get up. They
assisted him.

'I heard your call for help, sir –'

'You did a great job, Grigson!'

'But your son disappeared, sir, vanished like a ghost!'

'The hell he did! Call the guard! Did you call the
guard?'

179

'No, sir!'

'You're fired, Grigson!'

'If you remember, sir –'

'Go to hell!'

He staggered out, trying to orient. They had carried him to one of the bathrooms. Used to be Alice's bathroom. . . . And that boy, Alice's boy, for him to attack his father, he must be hypnotised, in the power of a killer, an assassin, the assassin, hiding out in his place!

He hit the nearest alarm button, was comforted as the unholy babel broke out from the clock tower. He took the elevator down to ground level, was met at the gates by Captain Harris, head of the security team.

'Didn't you see I was being attacked over the bugging, Captain?'

'No, sir! Where were you?'

'In the west wing, could have been killed! What were your men doing?'

'Your son removed all the bugging in that part of the house.'

'Of course, he would have done. . . . Listen, Captain, get hold of my son. Don't hurt him, but hold him. Lock him up safe down here. He is sheltering the President's assassin. Yes, you heard me! Get that assassin if you have to burn the place down. No, no, don't do that! Have a man go straight and guard my study, in case anyone tries to get in there and wreck my work.'

Harris nodded curtly. He lived for crisis. He issued orders all round, despatched men efficiently, told Byrnes, 'All shuttering is down, sir, and all doors are on autolock. Nobody can get out without our say so.'

'Okay.' He was mollified at last, thanking God inwardly for Harris; little Harris cared about the future, but he was great for emergencies. 'Then let me out of here, will you? I need fresh air.'

Harris deputed a younger man, who opened up the armourplated front door and let Byrnes through. He staggered out and sat on his top step as the door closed

180

behind him. He shielded his eyes and tried to calm his heartbeat, afraid of a stroke. His throat ached. The boy had hurt him.

It was growing dark. A dreary evening, the whole landscape. Macbeth-coloured, over the hills anger and unholiness. Good things of day began to droop and drowse. A searchlight came on over the lake on the landing-field, picking him out. He stood up, feeling guilty and vulnerable, signalling to them to turn it off. The great eye did not waver. Byrnes fought an urge to hammer at the door behind him for readmittance.

His little English sports car stood by the house. Muttering angrily, he climbed in, started up, and drove across to the field, the beam following him all the way. They must have identified him, for a figure ran from the guard tower to meet him. It was Captain MacGregor, to whom Byrnes addressed a blistering stream of abuse.

'I'm sorry about that, sir,' said MacGregor, without sounding very penitent. 'Captain Harris explained the situation to me over the phone. We have an alert on out here. But Secretary of State Crompton just radioed, sir.'

It was going to be bad. From men in office, full of ambition, only the worst could be expected. Death in their mouth and in their eyes dust. 'Well?'

'He said your son is charged with murder, sir, and you are charged with complicity, sir.'

'Washington madness! Madness!'

'He didn't radio from Washington, sir. He is flying over here, should be landing in eight minutes. Has strong police escort. Two planes. He ordered me personally to place you and your son under arrest, sir.'

'MacGregor!'

'Sir?'

'I order you to shoot those planes down.'

'Shoot . . . I can't, sir!'

'The future, man! The future demands it! Shoot them down!'

'I can't do that, sir. But equally I can't arrest you, sir.

181

You're free till they land here, sir. It gives you seven or eight minutes to get away.'

So MacGregor already judged him guilty. There was nothing he could do.

'Thanks, MacGregor.'

He walked away, past the sports car, the engine of which still ran quietly, heading blindly towards the bamboo grove. So much for philosophy. That fool, Russell. . . . So he and Marlo were to be made national scapegoats. A clever idea, certainly; much better than nabbing a complete unknown; they could fake it to look as if he had been after the Presidential seat himself, maybe – any madness they cared to dream up.

Miriam must have found out that Marlo was sheltering the assassin and had gone and told Russell Crompton. He would make political capital out of it.

Rhoda took his hand and said, 'I'm here, Jake. Don't be alarmed.'

'You, Rhoda? You here? What are you doing at Gondwana?' The balm was still pouring from her, a lovely womanly emanation. She was standing on the spot where he had earlier fired at his own image; perhaps just a coincidence.

'I am on your side entirely, Jake. The future's side. I believe as you do that the world can only solve its problems by throwing them open and facing them, not by suppressing them. I also believe that it needs all the forces it can muster to do that, and that among those forces you personally are important – *and* that you will be lost, and your book with you, if you do not ride out this next ten minutes. I'll help on that. I know what is going to happen.'

'Maybe you do.'

' "Here upon this bank and shoal of time, we'll jump the life to come". But perhaps it invites ill-luck to quote Lady Macbeth!'

'Rhoda . . . is the *haragei* gone? Can we speak and move freely together at last?'

182

'We can. I was not myself. Now I am.'

'Well, I'm beside myself! I get only chill feelings from all but you. Maybe we should cease to believe in logical systems at the expense of all others. After all, machines are now freeing us from the necessity of either – or thought; that's their job; we should deal with the nuances, where real life lives. I intuit that Russell is going to make me a scapegoat on the national scale.'

She nodded and said coolly, 'You realise that you are on the brink of madness. You must draw back. Russell has little against you save the guilt he feels for lying with your wife; but he has great ambition. To capture you and Marlo tonight and brand you with conspiring to kill the President would make him a national hero.'

In the darkening sky, the sound of engines. The new jet-copters. Yes, their lights visible overhead. The birds of vengeance settling on the tender plains of peace.

'I must go to Marlo. He's mad! They must not hurt him!'

'Think. You are rejecting the evidence of your senses, preferring to embrace sickness rather than face truth. You saw Marlo vanish. You must admit that to yourself; and then you just admit another thing . . . '

The darkness seemed to torment him. Angrily he shook his great grey head about, scattering tears. Trembling, he forced himself to say, ' . . . That he is the assassin.'

For a moment he could not see. The bamboos boiled like a midnight ocean and her words could scarcely reach him.

'Though the forces ranged against life are many, the thoughts of good always rise higher. Listen, my dear old battered Jake, you might clear yourself of complicity, but the disgrace would wreck you, break your life, disrupt the whole future course of events.'

The copters were crawling down in their own winds now. She was shouting to make him hear. 'I waited here for you because here you will see Marlo at any minute. He cannot maintain himself in the Lunar Automatic for long.

183

He will run to shoot Russell, who – with Miriam's aid – has pieced together most of the information he needs for an arrest. Marlo has immense powers, but he is not supernatural. You do not need a silver bullet, Jake, to bring a better future into being.'

He stared into her face. 'You know I can't kill him, my son!'

She kissed him on the lips. 'You will.'

As the wind whipped round them and the two black shapes of flight began to straddle the field, she pointed. 'Your Captain Harris was too late with his lock-in! Marlo was already outside!'

Forgetting her, he hurried towards his son, a dark figure running at a crouch, using the dead ground behind the sports car to approach the machines now landing. He shouted, but Marlo did not hear. He grabbed him from behind.

To his sudden fear, he saw the knife in Marlo's hand and the blank stare in his eyes. A man like a machine, not so much sick as unable to feel human or feel for humanity. As the knife came round, Byrnes saw that Rhoda, calling aloud his own creed, was right: it was kill or be killed. Even so, he could not kill his own son: even survival had a relative value. He fired the gun down into the ground, three times, as fast as he could pull the trigger. It diverted Marlo only slightly. As the knife cut his side, Byrnes jumped on the boy's instep and punched him hard and wildly under the jaw. They tumbled to the wind-lashed ground together.

Jacob Byrnes refused to stay in the local hospital for more than a day. Bandaged tight, he got himself driven back to Gondwana Hills as soon as possible. A benevolent – a highly-charged and erotic – image told him that Rhoda Crompton would be there.

As his driver helped him out of the car, Byrnes glared loweringly round. Work on the squash court had ceased, so there were no décor men about. But an Army plane on the landing-field, five big limousines, two police vans, and a mobile forensic laboratory told him that he had visitors. They would be taking poor Marlo's quarters apart, gathering every shred of evidence for the trial – in which, judging by yesterday's news reports, his father was going to be a sort of national hero as well as one of the chief witnesses. The wretched business would involve a colossal interruption of work; he thought he could face that if Rhoda were around. His main efforts must be devoted to trying to help Marlo. Miriam could be helped through solicitors. Feeding drugs to the boy, feeding him drugs! – that took some forgiving!

At the top of the steps, Grigson met him.

'Mrs Russell Crompton is inside, sir.'

'Didn't expect to see you still here, Grigson.'

'No, sir. But I thought you might have special need of me over the next few months, in view of which I feel I should postpone my resignation a while.'

He clapped his secretary on the shoulder. 'We need you, Grigson. Help keep the cops out of my hair. We may need your dangerous briefcase again for all I know. Come along!'

But Grigson faded away in the hall, muttering excuses, as Rhoda appeared. She had parachuted in, and was carrying a pair of goggles in one hand, although she had changed into a corduroy dress. Her long ash hair was pulled into a single braid, which hung over one shoulder. Cutting through any reserve Byrnes might be feeling, she put her hands on his upper arm.

'You won't be surprised to see me, but I hope you're pleased. I figured you needed help here for a while.'

'Everyone seems to think I need help. How intuitive everyone has suddenly become! Come on upstairs, Rhoda, before I go and talk to the cops. You can make me a drink; that damned hospital was on a temperance kick.'

'How's the side?'

'It was a love bite.' He looked at her, smiled, hoping he

did not look too tired and old; she seemed to find a question in his gaze.

'I've finished with Russell,' she said. 'He, of course, has finished with Miriam, having got what use he can from her, so I suppose the situation is symmetrical.'

'I ruined Miriam's life. I was too much for her. She's my responsibility; there is still help I can give – particularly now Marlo is off my hands. . . . Rhoda, do they . . . they don't make too much of a godamned psychodrama of his trial, do they, purgation of national guilt and all that?'

She laughed. 'I cannot foretell the future now. You defeated the predicted future the day before yesterday by not killing Marlo. So the laws of temporal causation must be reformulated – clearly *have* been reformulated in the time ahead of mine, as is shown by the way nobody travels back to a non-time-travelling age, for fear of altering temporal causation.'

They took the elevator up to Byrnes' suite of rooms where he lived and worked. He still felt shy with her, had not entirely shed the feeling of *haragei*; he was inhibited from asking her directly what role she was going to play in his life. Knowing he was now, however undeservedly, a national hero for having tackled and disarmed his assassin son, he felt his freedom curtailed. At least he could use the popularity while it lasted to promulgate the ideas he stood for. First, he must confer with Fetesti; Rhoda should sit in on that.

'You are going to be so necessary, Rhoda. . . . Not just personally. You don't have to . . . return to whenever it is? You can stay?'

Colouring, she said, 'Don't count on me too much, Jake. I love you, but I'm a sky-diver and that's my first love – a sort of celestial junkie, you see. But I'll live here if you'll have me. Your drop-zone is second to none.'

She looked tenderly at the emotional warmth that crept into his face, then turned to get him a stiff drink as he sank into a chair, saying as she did so, 'I have no place ahead. I was born thirty-eight years ago; the future that kidnapped me during one of my sky-dives was only twenty years ahead.'

'It must be very different.'

'Tremendously. And yet *you* would recognise it, if only because a small part lies already in your brain.' Should she go on and tell him? There were reservations in people private even from themselves; she feared that what she was going to say might shock and startle him; but while it was his personal gun-and-clock time, so late in his life, he should have it straight. 'Jake, while they were training me for this – adventure, they gave me the Surviva inoculations, a variety of the Surviva inoculations mentioned in that fatal memorandum to the late President. I'm not . . . not subject to the usual three score years and ten any more.'

There was a long silence in the room.

Finally, he scratched the top of his head and said, 'People like you should always have the chance of a long, long life. I suppose that – twenty years ahead – I wasn't still lumbering around, doing good, holding forth, pontificating, was I?'

' . . . No. Your book was still holding forth, though, and doing good.'

'Give us that drink! Then I don't have to decide; the decision has been taken. I don't want the inoculations. The trajectory of my life is something I refuse to wrench out of its pattern for anything.' Then suddenly he was frightened at what he had said. He had done too much, suffered too much, and more of that to be got through yet, of course. The pain of Marlo's trial . . .

She kissed him as she handed him the glass. Suddenly he grabbed her with all his strength, only to release her, groaning.

'My side! I'll have at you, woman, when I'm healed.'

'I hope so. Here's looking at you!'

'And you!' There was so much he wanted to ask. . . . That inestimable privilege, never before granted to any mortal, of being able to look coolly ahead to the evolving future. He must not abuse it, must take it in digestible portions. One of the first questions will have to be – maybe he should make a list – how they managed to square the population explosion with having people around for longer, if the world was not going to be unbearably clogged with living bodies. But, of course, if they adopted the only possible system and gave Surviva free to everyone proved capable of benefiting from extra years (and what sort of test would that be, O Lord!), then it needed only another serum mixed with the inoculations to guarantee that the immortals did not procreate, or only to a controlled degree. The technical problems were not so great; it was the social problems that loomed so very large. Even a better politico-economic system would change so much, the wars of aggression, the famines in one state while there were gluts in another. Since world decisions were now going to be made, and the future was once more out of the log-pile, then clearly human consciousness was again on the dynamic upgrade towards a higher level of being. Longevity fitted naturally into the pattern. The pattern! Of course, that was what must be grasped – and could be grasped once the basic principle was taken; and the basic principle was so simple that the most backward African tribe embraced it whole-heartedly: life is good. And the clamour that would wake any day when Crompton announced the Surviva findings would show the west what the west had forgotten: that even sickness was precious, but life was better. Proof and proposition were all one; or to put it another way . . .

'Darling, you aren't drinking your drink!'

'I just want to make a note of something,' he said.

THE END

BIBLIOGRAPHICAL

'Neanderthal Planet' is a rewritten version of 'A Touch of Neanderthal' (*Science Fiction Adventures* §16, 1960)

'Randy's Syndrome' appeared in *The Magazine of Fantasy and Science Fiction*, April 1967.

'Send Her Victorious' appeared in *Amazing*, June 1968.

'Intangibles Inc.' appeared in *Science Fantasy* §33, 1959.

'Since The Assassination' has not been previously published.

Here, for the connoisseur, for the devotee of the SF genre, and for those who like their reading to combine excitement with good writing, is the Corgi SF Collector's Library – a series that brings, in uniform edition, many of the Greats of SF – standard classics, contemporary prizewinners, and controversial fiction, fantasy, and fact . . .

DANDELION WINE by RAY BRADBURY

Is set in the strange world of Green Town, Illinois, where there was a junkman who saved lives; a pair of shoes that could make you run as fast as a deer; a human time machine; a wax witch that could tell real fortunes; and a man who almost destroyed happiness by building a happiness machine. But there was also a twelve-year-old boy named Douglas Spaulding, who found himself very much at home in this extraordinary world . . .

0 552 09882 5 – 45p

BILLION YEAR SPREE by BRIAN ALDISS

BILLION YEAR SPREE is a comprehensive history of science fiction by Brian Aldiss, one of the genre's leading authors. From early works such as H. G. Wells's *War of the Worlds* to Kubrick's film of *2001*, sf has encompassed prediction, escapism, satire, social fiction, surrealism and propaganda both for and against technology. BILLION YEAR SPREE begins at the very birth of sf, with Mary Godwin Shelley's creation *Frankenstein Or, The Modern Prometheus*, and studies the growth and development of the media to its present successful position in contemporary literature.

0 552 09805 1 – 60p

THE DOORS OF HIS FACE, THE LAMPS OF HIS MOUTH by ROGER ZELAZNY

A collection of fifteen stories of man in the future, ranging in time from a few decades to a few millenia into the future, in setting from the solar system to deepest space. The prize-winning title story is the highly imaginative and very believable tale of a fishing expedition for an enormous sea monster under the oceans of the planet Venus; the rest of the collection maintains the high standard thus set, with tales of a rebellious preacher's son finding a different religion on Mars, of an expedition to an electrically-haunted mountain where a girl is discovered in hibernation state awaiting the discovery of a cure for her fatal disease, and of man's penchant for aggrandizement. All display the style, wit, imagination which have made Roger Zelazny one of the most highly praised writers of science fiction today.

0 552 10021 8 – 50p

THE FLYING SORCERERS by DAVID GERROLD and LARRY NIVEN

SHOOGAR was absolutely livid – a natural state for any self-respecting witch-doctor . . .

But this time he had a reason. His territory had been invaded by a completely insane shaman who hadn't had the grace to announce himself and didn't even appear to know the common ground rules of the magicians' guild. And what's more, the idiot dared to practise witchcraft without having first made his gift to the local witch-doctor, who happened to be the mighty Shoogar . . .

In an absolute fury Shoogar prepared his most ghastly spells to drive the foreigner away . . . little did he know that the stranger had quite a few ghastly spells of his own to fall back on . . .

0 552 09907 4 – 60p

A SELECTED LIST OF CORGI SCIENCE FICTION FOR YOUR READING PLEASURE

☐ 09824 8	NEQ THE SWORD	Piers Anthony	40p
☐ 09731 4	SOS THE ROPE	Piers Anthony	40p
☐ 09736 5	VAR THE STICK	Piers Anthony	40p
☐ 09080 8	STAR TREK 1	James Blish	30p
☐ 09081 6	STAR TREK 2	James Blish	25p
☐ 09082 4	STAR TREK 3	James Blish	25p
☐ 09445 5	STAR TREK 4	James Blish	30p
☐ 09446 3	STAR TREK 5	James Blish	30p
☐ 09447 1	STAR TREK 6	James Blish	30p
☐ 09229 0	STAR TREK 7	James Blish	30p
☐ 09498 6	SPOCK MUST DIE!	James Blish	30p
☐ 08775 9	MACHINERIES OF JOY	Ray Bradbury	30p
☐ 09765 9	THE HALLOWEEN TREE	Ray Bradbury	60p
☐ 09492 7	NEW WRITINGS IN S.F.22	ed. Kenneth Bulmer	35p
☐ 09681 4	NEW WRITINGS IN S.F.23	ed. Kenneth Bulmer	40p
☐ 09554 0	NINE PRINCES IN AMBER	Roger Zelazny	35p
☐ 09608 3	JACK OF SHADOWS	Roger Zelazny	35p

CORGI SF COLLECTOR'S LIBRARY

☐ 09237 1	FANTASTIC VOYAGE	Isaac Asimov	35p
☐ 09784 5	THE SILVER LOCUSTS	Ray Bradbury	40p
☐ 09238 X	FAHRENHEIT 451	Ray Bradbury	45p
☐ 09706 3	I SING THE BODY ELECTRIC	Ray Bradbury	45p
☐ 09333 5	THE GOLDEN APPLES OF THE SUN	Ray Bradbury	40p
☐ 09413 7	REPORT ON PLANET THREE	Arthur C. Clarke	40p
☐ 09473 0	THE CITY AND THE STARS	Arthur C. Clarke	40p
☐ 09236 3	DRAGONFLIGHT	Anne McCaffrey	35p
☐ 09474 9	A CANTICLE FOR LEIBOWITZ	Walter M. Miller Jr.	45p
☐ 09414 5	EARTH ABIDES	George R. Stewart	35p
☐ 09239 8	MORE THAN HUMAN	Theodore Sturgeon	35p

All these books are available at your bookshop or newsagent; or can be ordered direct from the publisher. Just tick the titles you want and fill in the form below.

CORGI BOOKS, Cash Sales Department, P.O. Box 11, Falmouth, Cornwall.
Please send cheque or postal order, no currency.
U.K. and Eire send 15p for first book plus 5p per copy for each additional book ordered to a maximum charge of 50p to cover the cost of postage and packing.
Overseas Customers and B.F.P.O. allow 20p for first book and 10p per copy for each additional book.

NAME (Block letters) ....

ADDRESS ....

....

(DEC 75) ....